POST GRAD

POST GRAD

Emily Cassel

St. Martin's Griffin

New York

POST GRAD.™ and copyright © 2009 by Twentieth Century Fox Film Corporation. All rights reserved. Printed in the United States of America. For information, address St. Martin's Press, 175 Fifth Avenue, New York, N.Y. 10010.

www.stmartins.com

Library of Congress Cataloging-in-Publication Data

Cassel, Emily.
Post grad / Emily Cassel. — 1st ed.
p.   cm.
ISBN 978-0-312-59626-2
1. Young women—Fiction.   2. Adult children living with parents—Fiction.   3. San Fernando Valley (Calif.)—Fiction.
4. Domestic fiction.   I. Title.
PS3603.A8683P67 2009
813'.6—dc22
2009010207

10   9   8   7   6   5   4   3   2

To Ben, the best brother ever,
and very nearly a post grad himself

ACKNOWLEDGMENTS

A great big thank-you to Katie Simon and Nicole Mc-Mullin, who saw this book through from beginning to end. Thanks, also, to my Californian parents, James and Betsy Cassel; my French boyfriend, Xavier Pompidou; and my English bulldog, Percy. And last but definitely not least, thanks to Joelle Hobeika, friend and editor extraordinaire.

POST GRAD

CHAPTER 1

"Okay, okay, next question. Would you rather be a mongoose or a platypus?" Adam Davies, my tall, green-eyed, only slightly goofy Best Friend in the World, gazed up at me intently from my dorm room floor, as if my answer to this question were a matter of earth-shattering importance.

I took a sip of the beer that I'd gotten from the keg down the hall and pretended to mull it over. "A mongoose . . . Well, that's a bit weaselly for me. A bit too much on the rodent side of things. But honestly, what is a platypus anyway? It has a bill, it lays eggs, but apparently it's a mammal. I mean, how does that work? What does it do with its life?"

"I'm not really sure." Adam rolled over so that he was peering under my bed. "God," he said, "have you ever heard of a broom? You've got dust balls the size of cats under here."

I threw a pillow at him and it landed on his broad chest. "Hey, I'll be out of here any day now," I said. "I'm done with cleaning. I leave that to the paid employees of Clarendon University."

He picked the pillow up and tossed it back but missed me. He threw worse than a girl; he always had. "So a mongoose, then?" he asked. "You'd be a mongoose? You'd have to fight snakes. That's what mongooses do. Or is it mongeese?"

We'd been playing the Which Would You Rather Be? game for fifteen years, ever since we were seven years old and swinging next to each other in Jackson Park in Glendale, California, while our babysitters gossiped on the nearby benches, drinking Cokes and eating M&M's (which they wouldn't share with us because they claimed the sugar made us crazy—which it did). You'd think we'd be bored with it, and maybe we were. But it was so familiar that we couldn't help it. It was something to say when there was nothing else to talk about, for one. Something to calm our nerves before an exam or a blind date—things like that. We just fell into it.

Lately our game seemed to focus not on the animals themselves so much as on what they did. For instance, you wouldn't want to be a dog, because you'd have to do what people told you all day long. You wouldn't want to be an ox, either, because those yoke things looked really heavy. And you wouldn't want to be a monkey, because you'd have to pick bugs out of your friends' hair all the time. And then you'd probably have to eat the bugs so as not to seem rude.

This focus on the animals' activities was because we were seniors in college, and graduation was less than eighteen hours away, and we had our whole lives in front of us. We could be anything. That's what we told ourselves, anyway. We could be mules—forced by other people to do what they told us—or we could be tigers. Needless to say, the latter sounded much better.

Of course right now I'd have to pick platypus, since that was the question. And because I'm not afraid of being weird. I mean, just look at my family. They make an egg-laying mammal that looks like a duck seem completely normal. But I'll get to them in a minute.

Adam frowned at me playfully. "You still haven't answered."

"Well, you got all distracted by the dust cats. Which do *you* think I'd be?" I said.

"Platypus, of course," he answered instantly, leaning back and propping his feet up on my hamper (which, unsurprisingly, was overflowing with laundry).

See? He knew me, unlike the other 472 friends I have— or that Facebook says I have. The truth was that hardly any of those people meant anything to me, but I wasn't going to delete them from my friend list. I liked seeing their little profile pictures on my home page, and I enjoyed procrastinating on my English papers by reading their status updates. ("Sarah Adams is walking on sunshine!" "Brad Adkins is super stoked about his new wheels!")

Except for one. Jessica Bard. I had to admit, I didn't like seeing her on my Facebook page. You know Jessica's type: pretty, smart, supermotivated. Like, she'd stay up all night to study for a test and still show up to class freshly showered, her makeup perfect, with a plate of homemade muffins for the teacher. Barf. Of course she was valedictorian. (And her status updates were the worst. "Jessica Bard got an A! Again!" Double—or make that triple—barf.)

But I hadn't done badly for myself in school at all. I'd be getting one of those nice little Latin phrases on my diploma: *cum laude*. "With praise."

So I'd been planning for tomorrow my entire life. I was about to enter the real world, about to get a job where someone paid me to do what I love, which was not, contrary to how it might seem, drinking flat Budweiser from a keg and trying to figure out what sort of animal I should be. It was *reading*. I wanted, more than anything, to be an editor of big, wonderful books.

I devised the plan years ago. It was called, very cleverly, "the Plan," and it was pretty straightforward. One: I would do really well in high school. Two: I would get a good scholarship so my parents wouldn't have to bankrupt themselves sending me to college. Three: I'd limit my games of beer pong and Never Have I Ever at said college so as to keep said scholarship. And most importantly, number four: upon my graduation with a B.A. in English literature, I would land a sweet job at the finest publishing house in Los Angeles (Happerman & Browning, FYI), so I could discover the next Great American Novel and marry Jonathan Micah Miller, who had become a literary prodigy at the tender age of seventeen with his bestselling novel *I Love Everyone and Everyone Loves Me*.

Adam downed the last swig of his beer and sat up. "You want another?" he asked, holding up the cheap plastic cup that said TIJUANA RULES, a souvenir all the way from our freshman-year spring break. (It was my only souvenir from that trip, and for that I was thankful—my friend Julie had returned with a tattoo of Mario Lopez on her butt. Needless to say, she'd been very, very drunk when she'd picked it out.)

I shook my head. I didn't want a hangover and bags

under my eyes on graduation day. "No on the beer, thanks. I need my beauty rest."

"You'd have to sleep a really long time to get beautiful," Adam countered. "I mean, you'd have to miss commencement and everything." But then he smiled. Because actually he thought I was pretty, and he told me so every time I needed a little ego boost. Because long auburn hair and blue eyes and good skin and a decent figure are nice, but everyone needs a little reassurance now and then.

"Well, good night," he said. "See you in the A.M., cum laude."

Adam let himself out, and I fell back onto my bed. I picked thoughtfully at the Ernest Hemingway poster on the wall and let moments of the past four years flicker in my mind in the form of a nostalgic film strip: getting lost in the library stacks, eating nachos in the dining hall, writing papers on Shakespeare and Faulkner, staying up late with Adam as we gorged ourselves on pizzas we'd microwaved in the dorm kitchen. College had been great. But I was ready for it to be over; I was ready to live on my own. And I was as certain about the Plan as I'd ever been.

Granted, I was eleven when I came up with it, so some of it had changed. For instance, I no longer wanted to marry Jonathan Micah Miller because, in the words of one book critic, "*two* names is enough for the rest of us, you dick." And he would be twenty-eight by now—no longer a prodigy! But anyway, I was three for three on my goals, and, as I prepared to be shot from the cannon of my higher education into the battlefield of the real world, I felt sure number four was a given. I was ready for the world. So the question was: was the world ready for me?

CHAPTER 2

Graduation Day dawned sunny and warm and golden. Of course, this was L.A., so the weather was not particularly unusual. What *was* unusual were the hordes of people who had descended upon our college. They trampled the grass, looking confusedly at their campus maps and yelling at their kids to stay close, and took pictures of everything, as if this chaos were something to be remembered and preserved instead of forgotten as quickly as possible with a very dry martini.

But the excitement was palpable in the air, and even Adam, who tried to be blasé about most everything, was giddy. He'd bought a new suit for the occasion, even though he'd known it would be hidden beneath one of the hideous maroon polyester gowns we all had to wear. In his silly cap, he looked like a boy playing dress-up.

"That's a good color on you, you know," I told him as we lingered in the shade of a large elm tree. "It really brings out the red in your eyes."

"Very funny," he said. He pulled out a camera from beneath the folds of his robe and took a picture of me trying to finish my chili relleno burrito before we had to file into the auditorium. "You've got beans in your teeth," he told me.

I waved this observation away. "I'll worry about that when I'm done eating. What I'm really concerned about is this ridiculous cap. It makes my head look potatoey, doesn't it?"

Adam laughed. "Potatoey? They're about to give you an English degree, and that's the best adjective you can come up with?"

I stood taller and puffed out my chest. "A cum laude English degree."

Adam knocked himself in the forehead theatrically. "Oh, of course, how could I forget?"

I couldn't help but feel proud—I'd worked hard for my grades, even if I couldn't think of a better adjective than "potatoey." As I finished the burrito and attempted to remove the beans from my teeth, I looked around at all of my

fellow graduates and wondered if they, too, felt such satis-
faction at the end of their college careers. I hoped so.

"So where's your family?" Adam asked. He pointed to
my mouth. "Still one more little bean piece."

"Thanks," I said. "I don't know where they are. They're
running late, they said. Which isn't really that unusual."

I was starting to get a little concerned, though. The ceremony was due to start in moments and they weren't anywhere in sight. I wasn't surprised—in my family, twenty
minutes late is on time, and on time is considered early—
but I'd thought they'd be able to organize themselves better than usual, seeing as how it was a pretty big occasion.
They'd said they'd meet me by the administration building at four, but then they'd called to say that they were
delayed because Hunter, my seven-year-old brother, had
refused to put his clothes on right side out until he was
bribed by a milkshake at In-N-Out Burger. (He claimed
that wearing one's clothes the normal way was capitulat-
ing to the fashion-industrial complex. Actually those were
my words. Hunter merely said he thought wearing clothes
the normal way was boring. But doesn't my phrasing make
him sound smarter?)

So as I scanned the sea of people, looking for my mom
in her favorite dress (blue with white dots), my dad in his
good tie (the only one without stains), Hunter with his
clothes on correctly (hopefully), and my grandma in one of

her atrocious hats (she had a thing for crazy chapeaux), there was a tiny, tiny part of me that hoped they wouldn't show up at all. That they'd decide they were having such a nice time at In-N-Out they'd stay there for the afternoon. And that they would opt to pay $49.99 for the videotape of graduation, which they would then watch in the den with a big tub of popcorn. I mean, I love my family, but sometimes I love them better when I'm not around them.

As Adam and I walked into the auditorium I felt butterflies in my stomach, just like I'd felt the first day I ever set foot on campus. Even though I was ready to leave, I couldn't believe the time had gone by so quickly. Four years ago, I'd never even heard of Willa Cather or E. L. Doctorow, never read Turgenev or Wollstonecraft. I'd thought that George Orwell's most important work was *1984*. Incidentally, I'd also never done a body shot, pulled an all-nighter, or lost my clothes in a game of strip poker, all of which were as important to my education as any of the books I'd read.

"Are you nervous?" I asked as I followed Adam down to our seats.

"Hardly," he said, tipping his cap at me. "In fact I'm already bored."

See what I mean? Congenitally blasé.

I felt a hand on my shoulder then, and I turned to see

Jessica Bard's Whitestripped teeth gleaming as she smiled at Adam and me.

"How are we doing, graduates?" she chirped. I noticed that she'd purchased a pair of sandals that were the exact color of our graduation robes.

"Great," I said, offering her a rather insincere smile in return. "You got your speech all memorized?" I didn't care whether she did or not, of course—I was just trying to be polite.

"Oh, I don't really believe in preparing too much," she said breezily, squeezing my shoulder and then reaching over to do the same to Adam. "I think it sucks the energy and intensity out of things. Plus I read a lot and most of it just sticks. So I think it'll be good. I mean, everything else about this event is so *canned*. I want to be spontaneous. An extemporaneous speech is the true test of one's intelligence, don't you think?"

I looked over Jessica's head at Adam, who rolled his eyes and then made a gagging motion. I tried not to laugh.

"I'm sure you'll be fantastic," I said. And I *was* sure. Because Jessica Bard had a freakishly big brain, not to mention balls that would make a bull jealous. And did I mention that in addition to being pretty, she also had a really excellent sense of style? (Barring those ugly maroon sandals, of course.)

"Well," she said, "I've got to be off. They're waving for me to come up on stage."

"Break a leg," Adam said. "No, really."

Jessica was impervious to his sarcasm. "See you two later!" she cried and strode up to the stage.

"Well," Adam said, watching her retreating back, "her speech will either be brilliant or total bullshit."

"Probably the former," I said glumly. It's not that I didn't want my friends to do well—I was thrilled for my roommate when she graduated early and went off on a Fulbright to Africa—but Jessica Bard was not my friend. "Look at her. She's, like, dripping with confidence. And her posture is perfect."

"I'll bet you five bucks the speech is crap," Adam said, and I shook his hand and told him he was on.

We found our seats and pretty soon the ceremony began, only twenty minutes behind schedule. It was your standard commencement, from what I could tell—there was a band playing and balloons floating gaily around above the stage. And of course there were people who'd decorated their graduation caps (I saw an alligator, a stethoscope, and what looked like a beer bong, each affixed to a cap on someone in my row), and I'm pretty sure I heard champagne corks popping in the rows behind me. And then it was time for Jessica's speech.

She was introduced by the short, squat president of our college, and she stood behind the podium as confidently as if it were her very own. She beamed out at all of us, a single yellow rose pinned to her gown. (Of course she hadn't decorated her cap—she was far too sophisticated for that.) "Class of 2008. It is my great honor to welcome you to today's graduation ceremony." I could almost see her breathe deeply, taking in the pleasure of being the center of attention. "I stand before you, classmates and peers, with optimism in my heart and passion in my throat when I pronounce to you two age-old words: 'carpe diem.'"

Adam and I exchanged befuddled glances. He raised his eyebrows up until they almost vanished behind his sandy bangs. "Carpe diem? Are we on the set of *Dead Poets Society* or something?" he whispered. "You are *so* going to owe me five bucks."

"Shhh," I said, not because I cared what Jessica had to say but because I needed to figure out which one of us was going to win.

Jessica smiled happily and touched her cap. "You must not see this day, or the days that led up to it—your classes, your exams, the papers you wrote—as preparation for real life. *Every moment of your life is real life.* Real life isn't starting now, my friends; it already began. So you'd better make the most of every moment. When we walk out these doors, I challenge each of us to not only seize the day but to clutch it with both hands, squeeze it with all our strength, and drain the victory out of every last living moment . . ."

"That's not horrible," I whispered. "The part about how every moment is your real life?"

Adam snorted. "Please. Cough up the money."

"I don't have it on me," I said. "In case you haven't noticed I'm not carrying a purse. And I don't have cash stuffed in my bra. That's my grandma's department."

"I thought she hid it in her hats?"

I giggled. "She keeps twenties in her hats, but any smaller bills go into her bra."

"What does she have against purses again?" Adam asked.

"Who knows." I sighed. "She's a strange old lady."

Speaking of my grandma, where was she? I wondered. Where were all of them? Was it possible that they really weren't going to get here in time to see this, my proudest moment?

I turned around, peering into the crowd, and that's when I saw them, picking their way across a front row in the auditorium, heading for a group of empty seats. My dad was clumsily edging his way past people's knees (and, no doubt, stepping on their toes), my mom was carrying Hunter—who is way too old for that—on her hip, and my grandma, who had moved in with us when I was still in high school, was bringing up the rear in red nails, powder-blue hair, and a hot-pink dress that looked like it belonged on a Real Housewife of Orange County. Oh, and she was also wearing a hat with a large red parrot on it. Oh, and Hunter was waving around this awful sock puppet he has, which Grandma made for him when he was three and which he calls Larry. Hunter loves Larry and takes him practically everywhere he goes, which is why Larry is always filthy.

I turned to Adam, cringing. "The crazies are here," I said.

"Oh, good," he said. "I was getting worried."

Adam actually liked my family, which was one of the reasons he was the Best Friend Ever.

Jessica blathered on up there behind the podium, something about how our generation was stronger, smarter, and better equipped than all those that came before us. And how it was our responsibility—no, our *destiny,* she said—to forge ahead and stake our rightful claim at the top of the pyramid of life . . .

Blah blah blah, I said to myself. Maybe I *would* owe Adam five dollars. But it was kind of hard to concentrate because I kept turning around to check on my family. They had settled into their seats, and I could see that my grandma, apparently under the impression that she was at a movie theater, had brought out a bag of Smartfood popcorn. My little brother was kneeling in his chair, waving Larry around, and at one point it seemed as if Larry were lovingly and inappropriately caressing the hair of the woman in front of him. (I seriously hoped my eyes were playing tricks on me.)

But I tried to stop worrying about them. Tried to pay attention to Jessica so as to settle the bet with Adam. Tried to enjoy the last moments before I was officially a college graduate. My attempts worked well enough, and pretty soon Jessica finished, our names were called, and Adam and I walked, single file with the rest of our row, toward the stage to accept our diplomas. (Which, incidentally, were not our real diplomas, but blank stand-ins in brown, fake-leather folders. Not wanting to be responsible for ensuring the correct student/diploma matchup, the college had simply informed us to watch our mail for the actual thing.)

Adam received his degree, along with a handshake from the president, and a cheer went up as he waved to the various girls who'd been such fans of his campus rock band, Captain Corduroy. The clapping was not as loud for me, but it wasn't embarrassingly quiet, either, as it had been for poor Tim Kelly, the guy from our row who'd majored in Special Nerd Math and had never been seen outside of the library or the dining hall. Anyway, I accepted my fake-diploma folder, took in the applause, and turned to smile at my proud family.

Which was when I realized that they had come not to support me, but to humiliate me. My dad snatched Larry away from Hunter, who began to scream bloody murder. My grandma removed her hat and began to use it as a very ineffectual weapon against my dad, which in turn made my mother try to throw herself in the midst of the scrum, clearly begging for them all to calm down.

Half of my classmates and their parents had also turned to watch my family as they behaved like a pack of rabid hyenas. *Kill me now,* I thought. *Just kill me now.* For a moment I closed my eyes and pretended none of it was happening. That's why, in my graduation picture—you know, the one they snap of you at your supposedly proudest moment—I look like someone who is about to pass out. And believe me, unconsciousness at that instant would have been a gift.

I walked off stage, head hung low, and went to stand by Adam.

"I can't believe them!" I cried, burying my face in his chest. "Can you believe them?"

Adam glanced over to the stands and said, "It's safe to look now. I think they've settled down. Hunter has that sock thing back."

"Larry," I said miserably.

Adam pushed me away and looked in my eyes. "Hey, at least your family came. My dad didn't even show."

I smiled faintly and put my arm around his waist. "You're lucky, then. Did you hear Hunter shrieking? Thank God I'm officially a grown-up now. I'm finally free of those freaks."

"You're never free of your family," Adam said, playfully tapping me on the head with his pleather folder. Little did I know how right he was.

CHAPTER 3

One of the things to know about my family is that they love Chinese food, and Chinese buffets in particular. My dad prefers a buffet because he can stuff himself to within inches of his life, and my mom likes them because she's a bargain hunter by nature and thus cannot resist the siren call of "All You Can Eat for $9.99." (Grandma and Hunter just love dumplings and lo mein.) So that's why we were sitting around a big pink table, pumping our bodies full of MSG, at the Golden Panda in Burbank. Or rather most of us were sitting. Hunter was hidden under the table, cradling the remains of his sock puppet, which my dad had shredded in a rage at the very moment I was receiving my diploma.

"And then in last week's class we learned how to paralyze a guy for life using just two fingers," my dad was saying.

He leaned over and jabbed his hand at Adam, who, like it or not, was basically part of my family. This was because, for one thing, I couldn't handle them alone, and for another, as he'd pointed out, his own father had failed to show up at commencement. And I had eventually managed to convince Adam that this was a blessing in disguise, considering just how inappropriate one's parents could be.

"And then bam!" my dad said. "Bam! Bam! That little maneuver and bang! Adam's got a parking space right up front at the grocery store and priority boarding on airplanes. You know what I'm saying?"

Adam, eternally the good sport, pretended to go limp and slid down in his chair. I thought he might go down below to join Hunter, but then he sat up and grinned at me. "Two fingers," he said. "Did you see that, Ryden?"

I rolled my eyes at him. "Yeah, wow, that's totally amazing."

"Anyway," my dad went on, "now that you're in the market for a job, Ryden, maybe you should consider working at the dojo. I could put in a good word for you." He picked up a dumpling with his chopsticks, gestured with it, and proceeded to drop said dumpling in his lap.

I leaned over to Adam. "Is he kidding?" I whispered. Even though I knew that no, no he wasn't. My grandma's shrill voice interrupted Adam's laughter. "A hundred thousand dollars on a college education and you want her to run around play-fighting with a bunch of Orientals?"

"Grandma," I hissed. "We don't use that word. We say Asian, or Asian American. And as you may recall I got a *scholarship* for my education." I took a bite of my dinner, the ironically named Happy Family. I suppose I'd picked the dish in some misguided moment of wishful thinking—I certainly wasn't a fan of "special cheff's sause" in general. It looked like weird brown sludge.

"We could also say Chinese or Korean or Japanese or Filipino or Sri Lankan or . . ." The rest of Hunter's contribution to the conversation was muffled, presumably in the mangled body of Larry.

My dad took another stab at a dumpling. "I don't want Ryden to fight. I'm saying she could help out at the front desk. Order the cinderblocks, make sure no one steals the stuff in the shrine. And we could carpool to work."

I tried to sound sincere when I said, "It sounds enticing, Dad. But I've got something else lined up."

At this point Adam leaned in helpfully. "So when is

that big Happerman and Browning interview again, Ryden?"

I smiled at him gratefully. "Monday at one."

My dad had succeeded in getting the dumpling in his mouth and he interrupted his chewing to say, "What's that? Happer-what?"

"Happerman and Browning," I said, enunciating very carefully. "It's a publishing house."

My dad swallowed and went after another dumpling. "How's the pay? Is it any good?"

"It's the best in town for editorial assistants." I watched as he chased the dumpling around his plate.

"Assistant? Hell, you could probably be the manager at the dojo. Still, though, if the pay is good . . ."

"And Ryden's got an in," Adam added. He, too, seemed fascinated by my dad's futile pursuit of the dumpling.

"Yeah," I said. "My thesis advisor is like best friends with the editor in chief, so he's already put in a good word for me and everything. Oh, and get this, they just built these incredible loft apartments a few blocks from the offices. They've got this totally amazing view of the city, and if I lived there I could walk to work."

My mother, who until then had been silent—she was making sure she was getting her money's worth at the buffet—finally chimed in. "That's wonderful, honey." She leaned down under the table. "See, Hunter, how success-ful and normal your sister turned out?"

"We could also say Thai or Cambodian or Vietnam-ese," Hunter said. I could see his feet peeking out from underneath the tablecloth. There was rice clinging to his socks.

"Well," my dad said, "I think this calls for a toast." He abandoned the dumpling chase to clink his iced-tea glass with his chopstick, and then he raised the glass over his head. He cleared his throat dramatically. "On this fine day, this grand . . . and illustrious . . . and momentous . . . and memorable day, I'm honored . . . and thrilled . . . and over-joyed . . . and pleased—"

"Two-minute cutoff," my grandma warned testily, steadying the parrot on her hat. "At this rate I could die before you're done."

Dad scowled at his mother. "I'm very happy to raise my glass to my daughter, Ryden Nicole Malby, who I'm very proud of."

"Ahem," I said, nodding my head toward Adam. I wouldn't bother telling my dad he'd ended his sentence with a preposition, since that would only provoke some disparaging remark about know-it-all English majors.

"And Adam," my dad continued gamely. "The guy who's sitting next to her, because we've known him forever and because his father was too busy to come and his mother couldn't make it because she's dead. We're proud of him, too."

At this point I put my head down on the table and considered crawling under it to join Hunter. I reached out and squeezed Adam's knee in a wordless apology.

My dad went on. "And on this wonderful, beautiful, fantastic day, I'm reminded of a story. It was a day just like this one, long ago, when Ryden and I were at Lucky's Miniature Golf Course. You know, the one off Wilshire? Over by—"

"Two minutes," my grandma hissed.

My dad sighed. "Anyway, we were at the final hole, the one with the gigantic windmill and the big treacherous moat that no one, no matter how skilled, had ever conquered. But little Ryden squared up to the hole, swung that club, and hit herself a hole in one."

My mom beamed at me. "We're so proud of you, dear," she said. "Not for the hole in one, though that was very good. I mean we're proud of you for today. For everything."

Everyone at the table began to clap, which attracted a few stares from our fellow buffet diners, and then everyone clinked their glasses together to toast Adam and me.

"Hooray for Ryden and Adam," Hunter called from under the table. "Larry and I salute you. Or what's left of Larry and I salute you."

I thought my grandma might have something congratulatory to add, but she seemed distracted—she was looking intently at a pile of fortune-cookie pieces in her hand.

"Grandma?" I asked.

She looked up at me from underneath her great big bird hat and frowned. "I think I ate my goddamn fortune again," she said.

I sighed and shook my head, grateful that I controlled my fortune.

CHAPTER 4

When Adam and I were in elementary school, we used to build forts out of boxes and chairs and blankets in my basement. My forts were always elaborate, sprawling things, complete with antechambers and hallways, while his forts were weird little hovels that two people could hardly fit into. This was because he didn't really care about building forts; he was just being a good sport. What Adam really wanted to do was bang on the old upright piano that we kept, for some reason, in the laundry room. I liked to think it was the beginning of his love of music, if music is what you could call his endless renditions of "Chopsticks" and "Für Elise."

Anyway, the point is that Adam never minded his surroundings much, whereas I always wanted mine to be as lovely as possible. Which is why I felt like I'd found the perfect home in this gorgeous loft, just blocks from the Happerman & Browning offices, with its floor-to-ceiling windows, recessed lighting, and gleaming bamboo floors. The apartment was certainly a far cry from my small, dark dorm room. Or from my old bedroom at home, which had cruddy pink walls and a unicorn, Pegasus, and horse stickers stuck all over the windowsills thanks to my equine obsession at age seven. (It was the whole *Black Beauty* thing.)

"Look at this," I practically squealed to Adam, squeezing my coffee cup in excitement and nearly spilling some of the precious brown liquid. "Didn't I tell you? Isn't it incredible?" I pointed to the wall. "Look. What do you see?"

Following my finger, he furrowed his brow and looked somewhat confused. "Um, drywall? White space? A place to hang your Sylvia Plath poster?"

I shook my head empathically. "Space for bookshelves. Space for all my babies, floor to ceiling. Organized alphabetically—no, by subject—no, by color of the spine—"

"Let's just settle down a little bit, Tiger," Adam said, putting a calming hand on my shoulder. "Don't move in just yet."

But I wasn't interested in hearing the voice of reason.
The loft was near Happerman & Browning, it had huge
south-facing windows, and white walls begging to be decorated. I could practically hear them calling out to me. "I
love it, I'll take it," I said to the landlord, an aging, very
tanned man wearing a Red Sox cap.

"Really?" the landlord asked. I hadn't even looked in
the bedroom yet, hadn't even poked my nose into the
closets. Which, he assured me, were very spacious.

"Really?" Adam repeated. He knew the rent, which
was not cheap. But then again, he'd be content in a dark
studio apartment with a view of an elevator shaft as long
as he could play his guitar as loud as he wanted to. (He'd
moved well beyond "Chopsticks" and "Für Elise," needless to say.)

"Yes." I sighed. "I can feel it. This is everything I imagined." I pulled the application form out of my purse. "See,"
I said, "I've already filled everything out."

"All right then," the landlord said, looking like a dubious, low-rent George Hamilton. "I'll just need a check
for first and last month's rent, plus security deposit . . .
So, four thousand ought to do it."

I didn't even blink. I whipped my pen and my checkbook out. Adam took the application from my hands and
gave it a quick look, and I could feel the skepticism radiating off him.

"Um, aren't you getting a little ahead of yourself?" he whispered.

"I'll have enough money soon," I hissed.

"And you wrote 'Happerman and Browning' under the Employment section."

I snatched the application back. "What are you, the apartment police? In a couple of hours, that'll be real, too." I glanced down at my watch. "Speaking of which, we've got to go!" I practically threw the application at the landlord and grabbed Adam's hand. "Thanks a million," I said. "I'm hoping to start moving my stuff in ASAP."

The landlord gave me a thin, insincere smile. "Just as soon as I call your references and your check clears," he said. Then he tipped his baseball cap at us.

Adam and I stepped outside into the bright Century City sunlight and I nearly danced to my car with excitement. "Ask me an interview question," I said, unable to resist a bit of happy skipping. "Let's make all this happen *today*. New apartment, new job, new life."

Adam gamely made himself look very serious. "Ms. Malby, to whom do you ascribe your desire to work at Happerman and Browning?"

"Well, sir, that's a good question," I said, climbing into the passenger seat of my blue Ford Escort (Adam had agreed to be my chauffer for the day in repayment for my editorial assistance on his final history paper). "I've always loved to read, and so I think the proper word isn't 'whom' but 'what'—and it was *books* that made me want to work in publishing, and it was Happerman and Browning's stellar reputation that made me want to work for this company specifically."

Adam folded his long legs beneath the steering wheel. "Okay, reasonable enough, though a little ass-kissy. Next question. Would you hit this?" He pointed to himself. "I mean, hypothetically let's say I'm the hottest guy in the world, and you pull up next to me at a stop sign, and this is what I look like driving this car."

His knees were practically hitting the dashboard, his neck bent so he wouldn't hit his head on the ceiling. He was wearing a faded oxford, untucked, and a pair of Bermuda shorts. "You ask me that every time you drive my car," I said, sighing.

"Oh, yeah," he said, "and I'm also making this face." He rolled his eyes back in his head and smiled like a maniac, waggling his tongue.

"Definitely," I said, giggling, "I would definitely hit that. I'm totally into guys who look like postadolescent zombies on Ecstasy. But seriously now, start the car, and let's get me to my interview."

Adam returned his face to its normal genial handsomeness and saluted. "Yes, ma'am!"

As he put the car into reverse, I asked casually, "So, did you hear from Columbia yet?"

He looked into the rearview mirror as he prepared to back up. "I got a big envelope in the mail the other day," he said. "So I don't know, I guess that means I got in or something."

My mouth fell open. I appreciated Adam's general attitude of nonchalance, but this was ridiculous. "What do you mean you don't know? You might have gotten into law school at *Columbia* and you haven't even bothered to open the letter to find out?" I paused and waited for him to defend himself. When he didn't, I barreled on. "Which leaves aside the issue of why the hell you didn't tell me, you loser. I thought we told each other everything!"

Adam shrugged and looked away.

"Oh, no," I said, jabbing him hard in the leg. "There's the shrug. You know how I feel about the shrug."

He shrugged again, still staring out the side window.

"Another shrug? I got the double shrug? Adam, if you want to go into music, just go into music."

He turned and blinked at me, faking innocence. "Ms. Malby, what experiences have prepared you for your work at Happerman and Browning?"

"Argh," I said. He'd always been good at avoiding things he didn't want to talk about. Things like whether or not he should play music or be a lawyer. Things about his mother. She'd died when we were ten, but he hardly ever even mentioned her. Sometimes I worried that one day he'd explode from all the things he didn't say.

"But really," he said, "this isn't about me. You have an interview in fifteen minutes. Tell me something about yourself. Give me three words to describe your—"

Suddenly there was an earsplitting crash, and the whole car lurched forward and banged into the curb. I screamed, clutching the dashboard, and Adam shouted a very bad word. Then there was silence, and we turned around to see an old pickup truck with Nevada plates disengaging itself from my rear bumper.

"Shit!" I yelled. "Shitshitshit!"

Adam held up his hand. "Shhh, it's going to be all right. Calm down. Calm down. You're not hurt, are you?"

I threw open my door. "I'm not hurt, but my car is," I said. "How am I supposed to be calm?"

He walked over to join me and we surveyed the damage: the smashed bumper, the cracked taillight, the wheel that suddenly looked as if it were facing the wrong direction.

"It's okay," Adam said soothingly. "His insurance will pay for it. Let me take care of this." He gave the driver of the truck a little wave and started to approach, the epitome of businesslike calm. That was when the guy gunned his engine, backed up, and peeled out of the parking lot.

"Oh, my God," I screamed. "What is he doing?"

"It would appear that he is perpetrating a hit-and-run," Adam said. Somehow, in his surprise, he managed to sound particularly mellow.

"We can't let him get away!" I pointed helplessly to the truck that was rapidly disappearing into L.A. traffic. Already I couldn't read his license plate number. I could, however, read his oversized bumper sticker. It said MY BULLS ITCH.

"Ryden," Adam said, coming to place a hand on my arm. "He's gone. I can't catch him on foot. We'll just have to deal with this later. Now get in, and I'll drive you to your interview."

I sighed miserably. He was right. There was nothing we could do about it now.

So I got back into the car and smoothed my hair and reapplied my lipstick to make myself feel better. And maybe things would have all been fine if Adam had been able to actually drive me to my interview. He couldn't, though, because, as we quickly learned, the car wouldn't move.

"Aaaaaaaaaah!" I howled, watching Adam try in vain to make my poor car work.

He twisted the steering wheel one way and then the other. "I think the rear tire's all messed up. Maybe even the axle. Do you have Triple A?" he asked hopefully.

I looked at my watch. There was no time to answer that. There was no time to do anything. If I wanted to make my interview, I was just going to have to run for it.

Which is how I found myself sprinting down a sidewalk in Century City in stiletto heels and a pencil skirt, my résumé in one hand and a MapQuest printout in the other. And by the way, if you ever want a bunch of people staring at you, that's a good way to make it happen.

But, by some miracle, I made it to my interview on time. I may have been sweating and panting, but I was at the receptionist's desk by 12:58. Two minutes early!

The woman looked at me curiously over a pair of hip black spectacles and pursed her ruby-red lips. "Ryden Malby?" she said. "A one o'clock with Human Resources Director Barbara Snaff? Lovely. Of course we're running a bit behind . . . around two hours behind, actually, so why don't you just take a seat over there and we'll call you when we're ready?"

She pointed behind me, and that's when I turned to see about two dozen other applicants for the job. They had their résumés in their hands, just like me, and they were all dressed up in their good interview clothes, just like me.

But they didn't look like they'd just finished a marathon, and they weren't ready to faint from lack of oxygen, and they eyed me with a certain unpleasant intensity. *Shit,* I thought to myself. *Shitshitshit.* But I squared my shoulders, smoothed my disheveled hair, wiped my sweating brow, and took my place among them.

CHAPTER 5

"So you just graduated, is that correct, Ms. Malby?" Barbara Snaff folded her hands under her chin and gazed at me with cool green eyes. With her sleek gray bob and canny expression, she looked sharp but tired—like she could use a double shot of tequila as a pick-me-up.

It was three o'clock by then, and frankly I could have used a little Cuervo myself. But I had been waiting for this moment practically my entire life, so I was not about to show it.

"Yes," I said brightly, "I—"

"Major?"

Okay, so she was efficient. "English, with an emph—"

"Minor?"

Make that *really* efficient. "Oh, communicat—"

"Internships?"

I took a deep breath. Maybe if I talked very quickly I could get more than four words in before she cut me off. "I did three publishing internships," I said confidently. "Byline, Wiltshire Print, and—"

"Carver Books, right, got it on the résumé. Any other pertinent experience?" She raised her eyebrows expectantly.

I twisted my hands around in my lap nervously. This was not going as well as I'd planned. "I was also an editor of the *Daily Bulletin* in college, I ran an online literary magazine for three years, and before that I worked on my high school's pub—"

She raised her hand to cut me off. "High school's not relevant for our purposes. So why do you want this job?"

At that, I sat up straighter and gave her my best smile. This was it. This was my chance. "Because this is not just a job to me, Ms. Snaff, it's what I love, and it's what I'm good at. When I was eleven and away at summer camp, when all my friends were swimming in the lake and earning their merit badges in archery and ceramics, I was hiding in my cabin, finishing *Catcher in the Rye*. When I was twelve I read *The Great Gatsby* five times. That sparked an obsession with F. Scott Fitzgerald that lasted all through high school. Then there was Bukowski's *Post Office,* the most explicit, inappropriate thing I'd ever come across. I was fourteen when I read it, and it was like sex ed, only beautifully foulmouthed. There was my T. S. Eliot period, when I chopped off my hair and took myself way too seriously—you know, 'I grow old, I grow old, I shall wear my trouser rolled,'—and then my Chekhov phase, then my Sexton thing, then Yates and Hemingway, and these days I love Alice Munro, Jonathan Franzen, Alice Sebold . . ." I stopped to take a breath. "I guess what I'm getting at is books are all I know and everything I love, and I want this job because I can't imagine ever doing anything else."

I released my breath, amazed she let me say that much without cutting me off. It was just what I needed her to hear.

But Barbara Snaff didn't even smile at me. She simply nodded briefly and stuck out her bony hand for me to shake.

"Pleasure to meet you," she said. "Thanks for coming in."

I walked out of the office in a daze, baffled as to how it could have gone so badly. As I looked around the waiting area, with its expensive furniture, its wood-paneled walls hung with accolades from the National Book Critics Circle and the Pulitzer Prize committee, and its lush flower arrangements—not to mention its crowd of waiting, wannabe editors—I felt almost as if I were watching my dreams slip away.

"Ryden?" said a voice. "Is that you?"

I turned to see Jessica Bard, valedictorian, overachiever, and brownnoser extraordinaire (remember the muffins), looking neatly coiffed and brilliantly capable in a Diane von Furstenberg wrap dress, the perfect mix of fashion and practicality.

"Jessica," I said, trying to hide my surprise, not to mention my displeasure. "What are you doing here?"

"They called me in for an interview," she said simply, as if it were the most natural thing in the world. "I like your hair like that. Sort of tangled and bedroomy."

Which seemed to me to be about as much of a compliment as telling someone their face looked kind of baboony or their ass looked really assy.

"Jessica?" Barbara Snaff leaned her head out of the hallway.

Jessica rushed over to her, right hand extended. "Barbara," she exclaimed warmly. "It's so wonderful to meet you."

I frowned. What was with the first-name thing? I'd been "Ms. Malby." As I stood there, watching the two of them smiling at each other, the reality dawned on me, and what I heard next just confirmed it.

"Dean Brunswick called me about you," Barbara Snaff was saying, "and I'm so glad we could fit you in . . ."

They turned and walked down the hall side by side like the best of friends. For the third time that day, I thought to myself, *Shitshitshit.*

Of course I should have expected to see Jessica here. She was an English major, too, after all, and a serious book-worm. But it seemed so unfair: four years of coming in second to her in everything, and now it was obviously going to happen again. If things went well for her at Happerman—and things always went well for Jessica—then she'd be the one to discover the next Great American Novel. No doubt she'd probably end up marrying Jonathan Micah Miller, too. And they'd be all bookish and smart together and live in some writer's retreat in Topanga and she could bake him her stupid little muffins for the rest of her life.

As I rode the elevator down to the lobby I crossed my fingers and wished for an entire stack of manuscripts to fall crashing down onto her head.

CHAPTER 6

Unfortunately, seeing Jessica Bard steal my dream job out from under me, thereby throwing the entire Plan into disarray, wasn't the end of the day's humiliations. That had come when I went back to the beautiful loft apartment, hoping to get the keys from the landlord, only to find him waiting for me with a scowl on his tan, leathery face.

"Happerman and Browning?" he'd said, scratching at a cheek as brown and shiny as shoe leather. "Funny how they told me that no one by the name of Ryden Malby works there."

So that had been that: my dream job, my dream apartment, all vanished in a puff of smoke on that bright June day. *Shitshitshit*. It was becoming the refrain of my life.

"Hey, Eeyore," Adam said, bringing me back to the present. "Why the long face?"

"You *know* why, you idiot." I leaned back in the plastic beach chair we'd pulled from the rack in the back of Valley Discount Foods, aka Adam's dad's grocery store. Adam was zipping up and down the aisle by the freezer section in one of those motorized shopping carts that all the grandmas use when they go shopping. (All the grandmas except mine, I should say. Mine shopped in high heels and carried a cane only so she could use it to threaten surly stockboys.)

"Here, have some more of this." Adam pulled a two-liter of Pepsi and a bottle of rum out of his shopping basket, poured a healthy amount of each into a plastic cup, and handed it to me. Then he dumped a bag of chips, a box of cookies, two bags of candy corn, and a big bottle of Tums on the floor by my feet. "Dig in," he said. "You are in a land of plenty, my child. Enjoy the bounty."

"Are you sure your dad's going to be okay with this?" I asked, reaching hungrily for the candy corn.

Adam snorted and spun his cart around in a circle. "Of course he's not going to be okay with this. But he does stuff that pisses me off all the time, so I figure I owe him." Then he got off the cart, leaned down, and took his guitar out of his case—did I mention that Adam rarely goes anywhere without a guitar?—and idly strummed a few chords.

Adam had definitely gotten a lot better since we were kids. I used to go see him in the student café on campus, and I'd sit there doing my homework while the freshman girls all drooled and swooned and wished he'd dedicate songs to them. That was his solo act—just him, his guitar, and a little bit of harmonica. His band, Captain Corduroy, was way too loud to do homework to. When they played, you just had to get up and dance. "Dylan?" I asked.

" 'Tangled Up in Blue,' " Adam confirmed, and kept playing. But instead of singing the lyrics he just talked to me. "You know that that Happerman and Browning gig wasn't meant to be. I mean, in some way I think this'll work out for the best. There are so many different things that you could do. No grouchy old human resources drone with a dumb last name like Snaff is going to be able to keep you down."

"That's right," I said, taking a big gulp of my drink. "It's fine; so what if it didn't work out as perfectly as I planned? Who needs perfect? Perfect is boring, right?" I was starting to convince myself. "I'll get another job. I've done the research. I'm a team player. I've got leads and—"

Adam laughed. "Don't you ever rest?" He reached into the freezer, pulled out a box of Eskimo Pies, and then tossed one at me. (He threw underhanded. Like I said, worse than a girl.)

I caught it and threw it back. "No, thanks."

Adam looked at me incredulously. "No, thanks? No, *thanks*? Are you actually turning down an Eskimo Pie?"

"Seems like it," I said.

"Have you ever had one?"

I shook my head.

"Then you are clearly unaware of the unique magic of the Eskimo Pie," Adam said, holding it aloft. "Did you know that every evil and terrible thing in the world is directly counteracted by the joy of biting into an Eskimo Pie? It's the only reason that the universe is still in balance and hasn't, like, gone into a supernova of bad karma or something." He shoved the frozen treat toward my mouth.

"Does anyone ever say no to you?" I asked him, accepting the pie.

"You do," he said, looking at me intently. "All the time."

He watched as I bit into the Eskimo Pie. I felt self-conscious, which is something I almost never feel in front of Adam—which is why he's my Best Friend in the World. But the way he was looking at me—I don't know, it just seemed a little funny. Like maybe he sort of wished he were the Pie or something. *Don't be ridiculous,* I told myself. *This is* Adam *we're talking about, not some horny frat boy.*

"Uh, yum?" I said. The Pie was pretty good, I had to admit.

He shook his head. "Pathetic."

Partly to be funny and partly to break the tension, I started to ham it up. "Oooh," I exclaimed, licking my lips. "Mmmm. Oh, yes. Oh, yes. It's fantastic. It's orgasmic. It's like there are rainbows dancing on my tongue. It's like nectar and ambrosia from the sun-drenched slopes of Mount Olympus. It's like God just gave birth to the universe in my mouth."

Adam grinned. "Okay, there's the girl I fell in love with"—he stopped and threw up his hands—"who has nothing but platonic feelings for me."

I tossed the Eskimo Pie wrapper at him. I never took him seriously when he said things like that. I mean, we'd known each other for fifteen years. We grew up playing capture the flag and building forts in my basement. We used to have spitting contests, and sometimes we dared each other to eat bugs. (Once I paid him a dollar to eat a spider.) How could someone who'd known me throughout my adolescence—through the whole pink-frosted-lipstick and permed-hair phase—really feel anything for me besides loyalty and brotherly affection?

I reached out and knocked him with the ball of my foot. "Silly," I said.

He caught my foot in his hands, and instead of letting

it go he slipped off my shoe and began to rub the sole. "God," he said, "your feet are freezing. It's like ninety degrees outside and your feet feel like they spent the night in the deep freeze."

"Well, we are right near the freezer section. But really, they're always like that. I have the circulation of an eighty-year-old man."

"So you'd rather be a flamingo than a penguin, I guess?" he said. "You belong in warmer climates."

"Definitely. Also I like the pinkness of flamingos. Plus, ever since *March of the Penguins,* all the penguins have gotten really big heads. They, like, want to have big Hollywood agents and eat at the Ivy all the time. They demand ice floes in the hotel swimming pools."

Adam laughed. As he pulled my other foot onto his lap and began rubbing them, I sighed with pleasure and leaned back in my beach chair.

"You like that, huh?" he asked. "Well, before you get too turned on here, let's not forget that you're not the slightest bit attractive to me anymore. I don't want a little innocent hand-on-foot action to go to your head. No, sir."

I was hardly listening to him. Feeling his thumbs pressing into my arches, feeling his fingers work their way around my anklebones—it was just so very, very nice. "So good," I moaned. "So good." This time I wasn't exaggerating the pleasure. Not that the Eskimo Pie wasn't good—it was very chocolaty and ice-creamy and delicious. But it wasn't as good as a foot rub.

After a minute I felt his hands glide lightly up my leg, tickling along my calf, and then slide higher. I froze, unsure how to react. Where was he going with this?

Just then a high, piercing giggle sounded from the back of the store. I opened my eyes and sat up, heart pounding. Adam raised his finger to his lips, and then he tiptoed over to the freezer case. He reached in and brought out a log of frozen sausage, presumably to use as a weapon. I held the bag of chips in front of me like a shield. My pulse raced as Adam crept up the aisle.

Two lurching figures appeared at the far end of the store, near the big rack of Doritos, and as they came closer, giggling, tearing at each other's clothes—I swear I could smell the booze on them, even from my beach chair—I heard Adam gasp.

"Dad?"

Mr. Davies looked up from between the ample, nearly uncovered breasts of his companion. His mouth fell open.

"Juanita?" Adam said, his voice rising. "Wow, I hardly recognized you out from behind the cash register."

Juanita, who I could now see was pretty and plump and half Mr. Davies's age, looked at the ground, embarrassed. "Hi, Adam," she said softly. "Nice to see you."

Roy Davies put his hands on his hips. "What the hell are you doing here?"

Clearly this was not the question to ask Adam, who was still annoyed at his dad for missing graduation last week, not to mention a little bit drunk, which can make him sort of belligerent.

"Funny," Adam said, "that was my next question for you."

"It's *my* store," Mr. Davies began. "I have a key and the right to—"

I could see that nothing good was going to come of this confrontation, so I grabbed Adam's arm. "Come on, let's go. Sorry, Mr. Davies."

"No, really, it's good to see you," Adam said sarcastically. "I mean, it's not like you're ever at home. So it's nice to run into you out with your little friend. No offense, Juanita. I think you're a nice person. It's my dad who's the prick. Did he tell you that he missed my graduation? Maybe you guys were on a picnic or something then."

Juanita shook her head, her eyes wide and nervous, and Mr. Davies walked toward his son with his hands held out in contrition. "You know I wanted to be there, but Albert and Rodrigo called in sick. Both of them! What was I supposed to do, close the store down? Where would Mrs. Alvarez get her frijoles negros? Where would Jimmy

Valentine get his lottery scratch-off cards? But look, I don't want to get into this with you right now."

Adam laughed mirthlessly. "Of course you don't. And you won't want to get into it later, either, I know that from experience. Well, have an awesome night, you two."

"Come on, Adam," I hissed, tugging at his sleeve. "Let's go."

He let me lead him away, but he wasn't done yet. He turned and called over his shoulder. "Hey, Juanita, if he's not giving you overtime for this, you're getting screwed. In more ways than one, if you know what I mean. Call the union. You have rights!"

After that parting shot, I got him outside. We'd left all that food in the middle of the freezer aisle, and I felt bad about it. But then I told myself that Mr. Davies and Juanita could finish off the rest of our picnic. After all, chips and candy corn always taste especially good when you're drunk.

I was sorry I'd finished off my Eskimo Pie, though, because as I watched Adam stomp through the parking lot, fuming at his father's behavior, it occurred to me that he could have used a bite.

CHAPTER 7

Of course, the Eskimo Pie has its limits as a feel-good frozen treat. Its pleasures certainly didn't last long enough to get me through the next day, which involved loading all of my worldly possessions into a U-Haul and driving them along a particularly miserable and trafficky segment of the Los Angeles highway system—*not* to my beautiful new loft apartment, but to my parents' olive-green split-level in the San Fernando Valley.

As if that weren't enough, my dad followed Adam and me in his dusty Suburban, towing behind him the body of my poor mangled car. As we turned onto Palm Drive, the wide green streets of my neighborhood seemed to mock me, and the June sunlight seemed especially harsh.

"It'll be okay," Adam said, smiling at me from the other end of the ratty U-Haul bench seat. "This is just a minor setback. The Plan lives on." He reached down into the pocket of the door and held up a filthy orange lollipop that had been left by the truck's previous renters. "Look!" he said brightly. "A snack!" He pretended to lick it.

I rolled my eyes. "You're disgusting," I told him.

My mother was waiting for us in the driveway, sympathy written all over her face. "You can stay here as long as you like, darling," she said, pulling me into an Anais-scented hug. (She'd worn that perfume forever because she'd bought an entire case of it at 70 percent off, and was still working her way through it.) "Don't you worry about a thing."

I shrugged myself out of her arms, feeling petulant. "As long as I *like*? I don't *like* it at all. Believe me, if I had any other options . . ."

Adam came up beside us and gave me a chuck under the chin, a sort of "buck up, camper!" kind of thing. I swatted his hand away. "Trust me, Mom, it won't be long."

She looked up and squinted at my dad. "Walter, dear," she called, "do you need help?"

I turned to see my dad struggling mightily to unhook my car from the tow. Naturally the curses were flying, but at least the volume was low. So far. I walked over and tapped him on the shoulder. "What are you doing? We still have to take it to the shop."

He ignored me as he attacked the towing mechanism with red-faced concentration. I didn't mention that the directions for disengaging the tow were printed right there in front of him—he was the "Let me figure it out myself" type. Which was admirable, you could argue, but also extremely inefficient.

Eventually he got the truck and the car separated, and then he promptly opened the hood of my Escort and began to peer into it, frowning at the engine with great intensity. After a few minutes of contemplative head-scratching, he walked around to the side, tapped the windshield glass, fingered the broken taillight, and kicked each one of the tires in succession.

"Hey," I said, picking a stray leaf out of one of the windshield wipers, "is this some kind of primitive diagnostic test you're running or something? Because there are professionals who do this. With, like, computers and stuff." *And actual skills,* I thought but didn't say.

But my dad remained silent, inspecting my car, and then the terrible truth dawned on me. He'd always considered himself the Mr. Fix-it type (see above re: the "Let me figure it out myself" thing), despite all evidence to the contrary. "Oh, no," I said, trying to pull him away from the car. "Oh, no, oh, no. You are not thinking of fixing this yourself."

He grunted and moved his hand down to scratch pensively at his chin. He was *clearly* thinking about fixing it himself.

"Dad," I warned. "No. You can't. I really need this car."

He finally turned to me, looking affronted. "Have a little faith in my abilities, huh, Ryden?"

I threw up my hands, helpless in the face of his determination. "But you've never fixed a car before!" I reminded him. "You don't *have* the abilities! Remember when you tried to fix the lawn mower and you made it so it only ran backward? I can't drive my car in reverse all over L.A., Dad. It just won't work. You can't do it."

"There, there," he said, patting my head like I was Hunter's age. "There was a time in my life when I had never roundhouse-kicked a man in the neck before, either. And now I do it every Wednesday, and believe it or not I'm very good at it." He kicked the rear tire of my Escort and then winced in pain. But he recovered quickly. "Ryden, your father's brain is like a sea sponge. It soaks up knowledge like plankton. You just can't keep those synapses from firing. Boom, boom! Bang! Bang!" He waved his arms around his head, miming firing synapses.

I slouched down, clearly defeated, and watched as my little brother came running up, clutching a flyer in his sticky little hands. He hardly even noticed that I was standing there, so intent was he on his mission.

"Dad, Dad!" he cried. "Can we build a box car? Can we?"

"Not now," my dad said, closing the Escort's hood. "We've got to help your sister unpack. As you might have noticed, she isn't moving into that fancy apartment she kept talking about. Adam, grab the other end of that blue thing, will you?"

Adam saluted. "Ready when you are, sir," he said, moving toward the blue dresser I'd had since I was five. It had sat in my dorm room for four years, and I had thought it would be moving into my grown-up apartment with me. Now it was being taken right back where it started. Just like me.

Hunter was not so easily brushed off. "Please! Please! Pretty please! The derby is in August."

"Don't say 'pretty please,' Hunter," my dad said. "You sound like a queer."

"Dad! Don't say that word!" I cried. I had tried—*oh, how I had tried*—to explain the concept of politically correct speech to him, but somehow he just never seemed to get it.

Hunter stood looking crestfallen as my dad struggled with his end of the dresser. Adam, I noticed, lifted it easily. I wondered if I could manage to get out of helping somehow. After all, I'd loaded it into the truck. Wasn't it someone else's turn to take it out?

"He'll help you soon," I reassured Hunter. "He's just a little busy right now."

My dad proceeded to walk up the driveway, puffing hard and already sweating. Because he was walking backward with his end of the dresser, he failed to see the new neighbor's cat as it finished depositing a small warm dollop of crap right in the middle of his path.

"Hey—" I called, but it was too late. My dad's shoe landed in the middle of the pile with an audible squish. *That's what you get for saying "queer,"* I thought.

"Crap!" my dad yelled as the cat disappeared into the neighbor's backyard. He set the dresser down with a bang. "That goddamn cat did it again!" He wiped his shoe against the driveway, smearing the crap in a long brown streak.

"Dad, it'll wash off, no big deal," I said. "I'll go get the hose." I figured spraying cat shit off the driveway was easier than unloading boxes, so I didn't mind, even though it was pretty gross.

"No, that's it! It's over!" he bellowed. "That cat has shat

its last shit on my property!" He whipped off his work gloves and stormed across the lawn to the neighbor's.

"Stay here," I instructed Hunter and Adam, both of whom looked quite interested in the coming confrontation. "The last thing he needs is a big audience. It encourages him." I hurried after my dad, praying he wouldn't make too much of a scene. "Dad," I called. "Please calm down. Please just leave this poor person alone." *This poor person who has no idea that he moved next door to a bunch of crazies,* I thought.

"Yo, pal!" my dad yelled through the open screen door.

"It seems pretty clear he's not your pal," I said as I came up behind him. I touched the shell wind chimes that dangled from the porch rafters, and they made a bright, tinkling sound like little bells.

My dad stood with his fists clenched, waiting for someone to appear in the doorway. After a moment, someone did, and I drew in my breath sharply.

Our new neighbor was probably in his thirties. He had black hair and dark, mirthful eyes. Beneath his half-open robe, his muscular chest looked bronzed and smooth. He glanced from my pissed-off father to me, and then he smiled—a slow, sexy smile that made my stomach feel like it had been flipped upside down.

"Hello," he said, locking his eyes on mine. Then he

stepped outside and plucked the newspaper off his porch. I smelled Ivory soap and shaving cream and warm, masculine skin. "I'm David."

"Hi." I felt suddenly very shy. "I'm Ryden. I like your wind chimes," I added stupidly.

Walter held his hand up between us. "Um, excuse me, I hate to break in, but this is the third time your cat has crapped in my driveway."

"I'm very sorry," David said in a throaty, wonderful Spanish accent. "I won't let it happen anymore." He smiled at me again, as if to say, "I'll see you later," or maybe, "I wonder what you look like without any clothes," and then he stepped back inside. As he began to close the door in my dad's face, I tried to peer around him, into his house. Was that a half-naked blonde in the hallway? Was that the opening bars of "Let's Get It On" coming out of his stereo at ten o'clock in the morning? Just who was this Latin Lothario, and where was he all my high school years, when I had an uncontrollable crush on Mark Consuelos? And on Gabriel García Márquez, I might add, though my attraction to him was purely intellectual.

As the door slowly shut, my dad leaned forward and hollered, "You pretentious Argentinean asshole!"

"Brazilian!" our neighbor called good-naturedly.

That just about put my dad over the edge. I swear he started to snarl. "You—" he cried.

I yanked on his shirt as hard as I could. "Let's go home, please!"

My dad raised his fist at the unyielding door. "I swear to God, your cat craps on my driveway one more time and I'll run the son of a bitch over. I'll flatten that flea-bitten bastard, I swear to God!"

I finally succeeded in dragging my dad from the porch. He shrugged me off, straightened out his shirt, and wiped the rest of the cat shit onto our neighbor's grass. Then he walked over to Adam, who was still standing by the dresser, looking mildly shocked. "Ready to move this thing?" my dad asked.

"Yep. But Hunter ran off," Adam said. "So don't expect him to help carry the light loads."

I sighed. Poor Hunter and his boxcar race. No doubt he was locked in his room, licking the wounds of my father's latest rejection. Which is not to suggest that my dad was always mean to him or anything. He had a temper, sure— I mean, look how he'd behaved to David. But I understood why my dad might be a little fed up with his son. After all, Hunter knew how to push his buttons and enjoyed doing it. A few days ago Hunter had refused to walk, and had insisted on being carried everywhere, even from the living room to the bathroom. This had been specifically designed to annoy my dad, and unsurprisingly it had worked. By dinnertime, my dad forbade my mom to carry him anymore and said that if Hunter didn't want to walk to the bathroom then he could just go ahead and crap in his pants.

"Are you going to pick up the end of this thing or what?" my dad asked Adam, pointing to the dresser. "Look alive, look alive!"

And so it went, all afternoon. Adam helped, my dad yelled and cursed, and I—in between unloading trips— wondered more about that new neighbor of mine.

CHAPTER 8

What my mom had neglected to tell me when she said I
could stay as long as I wanted was that my dad, in a fit of
uncharacteristic optimism regarding my prospects in the
real world, had taken over my childhood bedroom with all
the crap he'd been collecting for the past two decades.
Thus, in the room I once called my own, there were: three
boxes of vintage beer coasters; two antique popcorn machines that he planned to refurbish (and which gave the
room the unappetizing smell of old oil and stale movie theater); a grimy fish tank with a single goldfish in it, barely
clinging to life; a handful of half-finished model airplanes;
and hundreds of little medieval warrior figurines clutching

spears and crossbows in their tiny, barbaric hands. Actually there was a lot more than that, but I'll just stop there.

Add on to that all my stuff I'd brought home from my dorm, and you had a recipe for postgraduate stress syndrome. I'd been unemployed for over a week, and enough was enough. There was only so much sleeping in and *Top Chef* reruns I could tolerate. Only so much fighting over the bathroom with Hunter, who, for a seven-year-old boy, was surprisingly dedicated to personal grooming. (Not that you could really tell—whatever grooming he did, he apparently wasn't very good at.) As I stood in front of my old pink-framed mirror—noting that my auburn bangs were in need of a trim—I held my own gaze and whispered: *I am going to get a job. I am going to get a job. I am really, really going to get myself a job.*

In the kitchen I made myself a cup of tea and spread the classifieds out on the table. It was old-fashioned, sure, but I wasn't about to leave any stone unturned. With a pen in my hand and hope in my heart, I read through the listings. What stood out to me right away was the fact that had I been a trucker with my CDL license, whatever that was, I could have had my pick of companies to work for. And if I wanted to try my hand at telemarketing, there certainly seemed to be opportunities there. Ditto medical billing and home health care. But I didn't graduate with an English degree so I could wipe some old woman's bottom, did I? I mean, I could pretty much do that around here if I felt like it. Not that I would, or that Grandma would let me. She was still capable of taking care of those sorts of things herself, thank goodness.

While I perused the paper, my brother sat at the other end of the table, enacting some fierce battle between two plastic action figures.

"Bam!" he said, making one guy smash a fork into the stomach of the other guy. "Take that, sucker! You think you're tough? I'm going to rip out your eyes and piss into your brain!"

My mother swooped over immediately like some permed, perfumed bird of prey. "Christ, Hunter," she said, grabbing the toys from his little fingers. "Watch your language. You're at the breakfast table."

"Yeah, but I already ate," Hunter pointed out, somewhat cleverly, I thought. "Also you just said 'Christ.'"

"You're not done eating yet," my mother countered, pointing to the egg-and-sausage sandwich she'd microwaved for him. "I see at least six bites left. And 'Jesus Christ' is not a swear word. He's God's son."

Hunter did not deign to answer her, but instead picked up the salt and pepper shakers and proceeded to engage them in a battle. I turned back to my classifieds as the salt kicked the shit out of the pepper.

.   .   .

After my mom had packed his lunch and gotten him dressed (shirt inside out, but really, did that matter?), she shuttled Hunter off to school. Then my dad breezed through the kitchen on his way to his managerial position at Luggage World, and my grandma headed out for the hair salon because she'd decided that her hair wasn't blue enough anymore. Which left me alone in the house, the only one with nowhere certain to go.

I made myself another cup of tea and pondered my options. There certainly weren't dozens of publishing companies clamoring for new editors, that was for sure. But after a few hours in front of the newspaper and online at Craigslist, I had a good handful of jobs to apply for—jobs that weren't Happerman & Browning quality, but at least they weren't telemarketing. I gave my résumé a quick proofread and then called Adam for a little reassurance.

"I mean, who says you should get exactly what you want?" I asked him. "That would be too easy. This is a learning experience, right?"

"Hmm," Adam said distractedly. I could hear him messing around with something on the other end of the line—a musical instrument, no doubt. He had all kinds of them, from your basic guitar, drum kit, and bass to xylophones, zithers, mandolins, harmonicas, and synthesizers. The only instrument he swore he'd never own was a didgeridoo, because, as he saw it, only neoaborigine poseurs played those.

"Are you paying attention to me?" I said, doodling "Hire me, Hire me" in the margins of the newspaper. "I'm looking for backup on this. I'm going to be okay, right? This is, like, something that will make me a better person? In that 'whatever doesn't kill you makes you stronger' Nietzschean way?" I waited impatiently as Adam finished fiddling around with whatever it was and finally remembered I'd asked him a question.

"Of course, Ryden, it's a learning experience, just like you say," he affirmed, and then was silent again.

I put my feet up on the kitchen table, something I wouldn't dare do if my mother were home; she had a thing against feet on eating surfaces. "Are you looking up the tablature for some Van Halen song or something?" I asked. "Because if you're too busy to cheer me up now I can call back later." I said this, but I didn't mean it. I wanted him to cheer me up *now*.

In the background I heard the faint sounds of an arpeggio coming from his keyboard. "Please!" Adam scoffed. "Van Halen? I don't think so. Bowie, maybe. But of course it's going to teach you something, Ryden. Think about it. Which would you rather be, a monkey or a sloth? The monkey has to work hard as, like, an organ grinder and whatever, while the sloth just lies around. But which one of them is happier at the end of the day? The one that got a big sack of peanuts for doing a good job, or the one whose greatest achievement was moving two feet to the left?"

I laughed. "I don't know what you're talking about," I said, wandering into the living room and flicking on the TV.

"I'm saying that you're a great worker, and you'll find something that suits you, I promise."

"So I'm not a sloth?" I turned the channel to Martha Stewart's show, a woman so preternaturally crafty she made Santa's elves look like sloths.

"No, you're definitely not a sloth."

"Thanks, Adam," I said, switching over to *Top Chef,* where the judges were trying to decide which aspiring chef did a superior job of wrapping bacon around something. "You make me feel better." (For the record, I would have voted for the bacon-wrapped figs. Not novel, perhaps, but oh so delicious.)

"To make you feel better is my one goal in life," he said, and then he plinked a few notes of "So Long, Farewell" on his keyboard and hung up.

I leaned back against the couch and grabbed one of my mom's *Better Homes & Gardens* from the magazine rack. As I thumbed through the pages, barely paying attention to the recipes for low-calorie desserts and tips for sprucing up a bathroom, I thought about how lucky Adam was. Even though he hadn't bothered to open the envelope from Columbia, I was sure he'd gotten in. And even though he wasn't sure that he wanted to go to law school, at least he had the option. So his future was not uncertain. And because, unlike me, he was a calm, sane person (I am sane—or saner than the rest of my family, at least—but I am not usually what one would call calm), he would be patient, and he would wait until the right time to decide what he wanted to do.

He'd always had that patience, even when he was a little boy. He was the one kid I knew who didn't eat his entire bag of Halloween candy in a single gluttonous night. He was horrified by my tendency to peek at my Christmas presents the moment they were set under the tree, and he always waited the full thirty minutes after eating before jumping in the pool. His patience proved useful in everything, from avoiding the stomach cramps and subsequent drowning that the lifeguards warned us about, to learning to play the guitar when his dad said he wouldn't pay for the lessons Adam so desperately wanted. Undeterred, Adam had gone to the library, checked out compilations of musical scores and books on technique, and had taught himself to play all of Johnny Cash's songs by the time he was thirteen. By fourteen he knew most of Neil Young, and by fifteen he could play anything from Black Flag to Sonic Youth.

By sixteen he was trying to teach me, because I had

become convinced that we should be in a band together and travel all over the world being groovy and famous. He would play lead guitar, and I would play rhythm guitar, and we would have a girl bass player and a boy drummer (or vice versa: the point was to keep the gender ratio even). We would all take turns singing, and we would co-write all the songs. It was going to be this amazing cooperative-collective thing. We had a long list of potential band names, which included the Hollies, Secret Service, Silence (that was Adam's idea; it never made sense to me), and Uncle Joey and his Barn Cats (that was mine; it never made sense to me, either).

We dreamed up logos and T-shirt designs; we talked about the tour bus we'd take from L.A. all the way to New York, and about how we'd never go on any four-lane highway, but keep to the back roads the whole time, so we could really see America. We would eat diner food and play impromptu free shows in dive bars and school playgrounds and in general be the coolest band that ever existed.

It was a beautiful dream. The problem with it was me: I had absolutely no musical ability whatsoever.

Most people who try for six months to learn three simple guitar chords (G, C, and D) will eventually succeed. (Most people learn them in about fifteen minutes.) But I was incapable of remembering which finger went where, and the few times I got the positions right it was sheer luck.

Any normal teacher would have flung up his hands after a single session with me, but Adam kept trying and trying, gently moving my fingers to their correct places. He had me singing scales and arpeggios, but as it turned out, I couldn't sing, either.

I think he would have been willing to keep teaching me until I got better at it, or until we both fell over dead at eighty, whichever came first. (No doubt it would have been the latter.) But finally I broke down and admitted it was hopeless. Adam would have to be in his own band, I told him. And pretty soon he was. And he was great. And I was always there to clap for him.

So now he was trying to decide his future, and as far as I could tell, either way would work for him. The law or the stage: he'd be great at both, and he could have the whole summer to figure out which it would be. And as for me? Well, I told myself that pretty soon I'd find *something* to be good at. I mean, how could I not?

My first post-Happerman interview was at Barer and Bostitch, a boutique literary agency with offices in Santa Monica. The woman who ushered me into her office was tall and thin, with a vaguely Olive Oyl–esque look about her. She glanced over my résumé, frowning.

"So you've never been on the agent side of the business?" she said.

I leaned forward and gave her my brightest smile. "I think you'll find that what I lack in experience I more than make up for in vision and drive."

"Mmmm," she said, tapping her pen against her perfect white teeth and then eventually biting it. It seemed that it was all she could do not to laugh me out of her office right then. She scanned my résumé again and then looked up at me. "Vision, eh? That's what everyone who knows nothing says, my dear. Call us in about five years, why don't you."

My next interview, two days later, was in the pink, flowery office of *Romance Reader Monthly,* the walls of which boasted large pictures of Fabio in his heyday, not to mention a dozen other male romance-novel cover models, all of whom had abnormally strong, clefted chins and large, oiled pectoral muscles barely contained by shirts that belonged in the *International Male* catalog.

I considered unbuttoning my own shirt a little lower, just to suggest that if romance was in the air, I was ready for it. But two things stopped me: one, I didn't want Louella Braverman, editor in chief, to think I was trying to seduce her; and two, honestly, my cleavage is not my best asset.

So, when asked about my work experience, I simply tried a line very much like the one I'd delivered at Barer and Bostitch: "I think you'll find that what I lack in experience I more than make up for in passion," I said confidently.

But Louella Braverman twirled her spectacles in her jeweled fingers, looking singularly unconvinced. "If one hasn't *known* passion," she said dreamily, staring into the void above my head, "how can one edit books about it?"

I nodded mutely. It was possible she had a point.

Interview number three took place at a coffee shop not far from the headquarters of Little Fry Literary Publishing. The reason we were in Starbucks and not the actual office space, explained Molly Fortunata, head acquisitions editor, was the twin boys of the editor in chief had come in for Bring Your Sons to Work Day and had set the copy room on fire. An automated sprinkler system had caused extensive water damage.

"So where were you before this?" she asked, brushing a stray blond curl away from her face.

"College, actually. But I think you'll find that what I lack in experience I more than make up for in enthusiasm," I offered.

Molly sipped her decaf grande half-soy half-low-fat iced vanilla double-shot gingerbread cappuccino with light ice and then smiled at me in a very maternal fashion. "What's your favorite young adult novel?" she asked.

My mind went blank. I had started reading Steinbeck when I was nine—what did she mean, young adult novel? Was I supposed to lie and tell her that I used to like the Sweet Valley High books or something?

"Um," I said. I wished I could think of anything, *anything,* besides Sweet Valley High and Encyclopedia Brown. "Wow. Gosh. I mean, there are so many . . ."

"Thank you for your time," she said gently.

My fourth interview, which was at *Motorheads Magazine,* was over about twenty seconds after it began, when I confused the terms "carburetor" and "alternator." My fifth, at *New Mew Review,* came to an abrupt halt when I made the mistake of telling Barry Michaels, the publisher, about my dad threatening to kill our neighbor's cat for using our driveway as a public restroom facility. My sixth interview was pleasant and collegial, but I was apparently not the kind of girl that *Holla,* aka *The West Coast's #1 Hip Hop Magazine,* was looking for. Nor did *Warfare Today'*s editor feel that my skills could be helpful to him. The publisher of *Colored Stones Monthly* took my lack of jewelry as a personal affront, and the head of *Domestic Textiles Weekly* suggested that anyone who could not define "grosgrain" properly had no place on the masthead.

Frankly, I'd had no idea that there were this many magazines in the world, and that I would be deemed unfit for all of them. I mean, when *Recycling Times* turns you down, where do you go next?

It was a Friday afternoon at the very end of June, and I was sitting in my umpteenth uncomfortable chair, having taken the bus to yet another interview. (Because no, my dad had *not* yet fixed my car.) I was hot and exhausted, and I'd just broken the heel on the pair of stilettos I'd been wearing to every single interview, not to mention spilled coffee on the pencil skirt I'd also been wearing to every single interview.

The human resources coordinator at American Insurance waited patiently for me to blot up the liquid that had just given me second-degree burns on my thigh.

"I'm just really passionate about the work your company is doing," I told her.

She picked up a pencil and tucked it behind her ear. "Really?" she said. "Like what?"

And all I could do was stare. I had absolutely no idea.

CHAPTER 9

"Snake or tarantula?" Adam asked.

I cradled the phone in the crook of my neck as I sifted through the pile of résumés and cover letters I was desperately trying to fax to any and all offices in need of entry-level employees.

"I hate snakes," I told him, pounding on the side of the ancient behemoth that was my dad's fax-copier combo. I'd read somewhere that fax machines were invented before the Civil War, and this one certainly looked like it had been around since then.

"So tarantula then," Adam said calmly.

"Nope. Snake. Shit, I think I just faxed a Domino's menu to *Bed and Bath Quarterly*."

"But if you were a snake then you'd hate yourself," he said.

"Hello!" I said, madly pushing buttons on the old machine. "I'm totally self-loathing these days. Unemployable and self-loathing. A snake is perfect for me. I should definitely be a snake and just lie around hating myself all day long."

He was starting to protest when my grandma wandered into the room, humming contentedly. She was wearing a violet robe and white bunny slippers and brandishing a label gun. I watched her as she affixed "Carmella" to a gaudy glass fish on the mantel and then taped "Walter" to the umbrella stand, which was made to look like the foot of an elephant.

"Hang on," I said to Adam. "Grandma, what are you doing?"

She turned to me, all fake innocence. Her hair was not its normal color of soft, old-lady blue, but rather a startling shade of periwinkle. (She went to the student stylists because they were cheap, and this wasn't the first time such a misadventure with hair dye had happened. Once she'd come home with hair as green as Easter grass. You'd think she would have learned her lesson, but apparently her miserliness trumped her vanity.) "I'm labeling things so you can all tell who gets what when I die." She held her label gun up proudly. "But I like this thing so much I want to be buried with it. See? I put my name on it, and a little note that says 'Keep with body.' "

"Oh, Grandma, stop," I pleaded. "That's so morbid."

She put a "Ryden" label on the fax machine and grinned sweetly. "Because you obviously seem to need this," she whispered.

I stuck my tongue out at her. "I'll talk to you later, Adam, I've got to go," I said, peeling the "Ryden" label off and tossing it into the trash.

My grandmother was not dissuaded from labeling things by my protests, and she was apparently having so much fun that she didn't stop at items that were hers. For instance, she put a "Hunter" label on the recliner that my dad had bought and paid for, and her "Carmella" sticker on my black leather Coach bag seemed to promise said bag to my mother. As if it'd be big enough to carry around all the junk my mother kept in her purse. I mean, the woman was a walking convenience store.

"Why don't you put a sticker on the phone, too?" my dad said, entering the room in a cloud of Aqua Velva. "Make it for Ryden—because the phone rings so often for her," he said sarcastically and handed me a stack of envelopes. "Special delivery," he said. "Your cell phone bill, your credit card bill, and your student loan bill. Oh, but look, here's something exciting. Your college diploma!"

Great, I thought to myself, *a lot of good that's done me.*

He walked over to the umbrella stand and kicked at the label on it. "Christ Almighty, Mom, what makes you think I want this hideous thing?"

My grandma skulked over and ripped off the "Walter" sticker, replacing it with one that said "Ryden."

Dad sank down in his recliner, looking weirdly happy considering he had just been contemplating the sad facts of his unemployable daughter and the eventual death of his mother. "The thing is, Ryden," he said, "I've got some very important news that concerns your future. I want you to pay close attention. Are you paying close attention?"

I gave up wrestling with the Paleolithic fax machine and sat down on the ottoman in front of him.

He put his feet up next to me. He was wearing sandals with socks again, though I'd begged him a thousand times not to. "I've got one word for you, kiddo. *Buckles.*"

I tore my eyes away from his foot faux pas and said, "Buckles? As in Buckles, the clown who stands out on Fairfax doing cartwheels and blowing bubbles for handouts?" For a moment I imagined that my dad wanted me to become the guy's understudy or something. So I could, I don't know, do handstands for a dollar. I could just hear my dad: "The money is all cash! It would be tax-free!"

My dad scoffed. "No. I hate clowns, you know that. Creepy bastards in ugly clothes. And those hideous shoes they wear! I mean buckles as in *belt* buckles." When I stared at him blankly, he continued. "It's a million-dollar niche business. They're selling like hotcakes on the Internet. I'm telling you, people are nuts about buckles. There's even an online magazine dedicated solely to the art of the belt buckle."

"You're kidding," I said, hoping fervently that he was.

"Nope, I'm totally serious. So take a guess who just met a distributor and is starting his own company? Your old pops. I'm going to sell them on eBay for three times what I'm paying the guy. Pretty soon I'll start my own Web site and cut out eBay's share. Make a fortune."

This was not the absolute worst idea I'd heard of his, but it was close. Also, I found it interesting that a man who literally never wore a belt—*I want to be able to expand after lunch,* he'd say—was planning on opening a business dependent upon them. "Does Mom know about this?" I asked doubtfully.

My dad waved the question away. "Don't worry about your mother. She's got her hands full between her work at the dental office and taking care of that nutty brother of yours."

"What about Luggage World? You're regional manager."

"I could care less about that place," he said, leaning back and folding his hands over his ample belly.

"Listen," he continued, "the point is, since all this other work crap isn't really working out"—and here he pointed to my stack of résumés and applications—"between you and me, I'm going to need to be hiring someone to help me run the business. I'm talking a vice president situation here." He raised his eyebrows and wiggled them, prepared for me to be grateful and amazed.

When I didn't say anything he leaned forward and said, "I'm talking salary *and* commission."

I didn't want to hurt his feelings, but this was *so* not what I wanted to hear. I'd rather clean toilets at the dojo than deal with my dad and his buckles. "Dad," I said, getting up, "thanks for thinking of me. But I don't think it's right for me. I mean, I'll think about it, but really, let's not get too excited about it right now. I'm really hoping for something better."

His enthusiasm was unaffected. "See ya later, VP!" he called.

I desperately needed to get out of the house, away from my dad's scheming and my mom's mad coupon-clipping (each week she took over the entire dining room with newspaper ads, store flyers, and a sharp pair of scissors), so I made Adam come and pick me up. He drove us to Eddie's, a bar that isn't really a dive bar but sort of pretends to be. You know the kind I'm talking about: neon beer signs, old jukebox, dart board. Eddie's also had twelve-dollar martinis and sixty different kinds of small-batch tequila, though, so it wasn't really fooling anyone. Once I'd seen Kirsten Dunst there with two bodyguards and a girl who looked strangely like Betty from *The Flintstones*. The people who were looking for a real dive bar went down the street to Frank's, which had two-dollar drafts, an old black-and-white TV, and plenty of beery regulars who'd look at a clean-cut pair like Adam and me with a certain degree of contempt and hostility.

"I'm going insane," I said as we settled into our regular booth. We'd been coming here for years, ever since our fake IDs got convincing enough. "My dad's going to be the death of me."

For once, Adam didn't ask me to elaborate; normally he relished tales of Walter Malby's missteps. "Mine, too," he said. He took the coaster out from underneath his beer bottle and proceeded to tear it into bits.

"Surely yours didn't try to rope you into some absurd moneymaking venture involving the Internet, a technology he barely knows how to navigate," I pointed out. "Surely it can't be that bad."

Adam gave me a wan smile. "No. It's just the law school

thing. Like, my dad won't tell me that he wants me to go, but I know he does. I told him I knew he'd hate me if I turned down Columbia. He says, no, he wouldn't—but that he just wants more for me. Doesn't it drive you crazy when they say things like that? It's like the ultimate pity card or something. Like his life didn't turn out the way he wanted it so he's after me to live his dream for him. It's so uncool."

.   "Did your dad want to be a lawyer?" I asked. I handed him my coaster so he could rip that up, too.

"Hardly," Adam said, his green eyes dark and troubled. "But he sure as hell didn't want to work every night until eleven o'clock just so he could afford the mortgage on a crappy two-bedroom condo in Encino and bone a cashier half his age. I mean, what kind of life is that?"

"He didn't actually say that, did he?" Mr. Davies had always struck me as the buttoned-up type, barring that one drunken night in the ice-cream aisle with Juanita.

Adam laughed mirthlessly. "No, I did. I called him out about Juanita and he said the saddest thing. He said, 'I manage a grocery store, Adam. I have to look for magic where I can.'"

I put my hand over my heart. "Oh," I said. "That hurts."

Adam looked at me ruefully over the pile of shredded

beer coasters. "It's funny. It's like our parents want what's best for us, and we want what's best for them, and none of us can get our shit together."

I thought about my family, and how it certainly didn't seem like they had their shit together. My dad was working as a suitcase salesman, my mom spent her days at a dental office, dreaming of going back to school to become an anthropologist, and my little brother kept getting in trouble at summer school for eating erasers, drawing all over his arms and face with Magic Markers, and telling everyone he was a marmoset monkey trapped in the body of a seven-year-old boy. And my grandma? Well, she dyed her hair blue and collected hats, and was perhaps the most misanthropic person I'd ever encountered.

But at least I had family. Despite their shortcomings, I loved them. There was safety in numbers, too: when my dad drove me crazy, I could go talk to my mom, and vice versa (though it was pretty much always my dad making me crazy). It seemed sad to me that Adam had only his father, who worked all the time, and an old bulldog they'd rescued from the pound who didn't like to go on walks or play fetch or anything. It seemed sad that they both wanted the best for each other, and that neither of them was very happy right now.

"But you got into *law school*," I said. "You finally opened the envelope."

"Yep." He took a long drink of his beer. He didn't seem all that excited about it, that was for sure, but I raised my glass and toasted him.

"Congratu-freaking-lations," I said, grinning. "I'd take you to a Chinese buffet to celebrate, but it's too late—they're all closed."

"And we don't really like them," he added.

I nodded. "There's that, too." I waved the waitress over to bring us another round. "Wow," I said. "Law school."

I didn't ask him if he was going, though, because I guess there was a part of me that didn't really want to know.

CHAPTER 10

My mother had taken pity on me and offered to drive me to and from some of my interviews on her days off, which was why, on a Wednesday afternoon in early July, I sat in the passenger seat, fresh off another failed stab at employment, feeling about as lame as lame can be. It was time to pick my little brother up from summer school—which he attended because he was "gifted and talented," not because he'd failed second grade or anything—and so we pulled into the lot at Evergreen Elementary and scanned the throngs of kids for Hunter. After a few minutes, I spotted him over by the fire door. He was standing by the principal, who was looking distinctly displeased with him.

"Again?" My mom sighed.

"Again what?" I asked.

She didn't answer. She just got out of the car and went over to talk to them. I couldn't hear what they were saying, but I could see the principal gesturing in frustration and my mother nodding her head in what seemed to me like an apologetic, vaguely annoyed way. Hunter was oblivious to all of this: he was staring up into the sky and spinning around in circles with his arms held up to the clouds. In his tie-dyed shirt, he looked just like a seven-year-old Deadhead.

After a few more minutes, my mom and my little brother walked back to the car, and she helped him buckle himself into the backseat.

"Hunter," my mom said gently, "you know I hate it when the principal is waiting for me in the parking lot, just itching to tell me what bizarre thing you've done today. What have I told you about licking other kids' heads?"

Hunter squirmed in his seat. "Um . . . don't do it?"

"That's right. Not ever."

"Not even if someone dares me to?" He looked up at her hopefully.

She shook her head. "Especially not then."

"What if someone pays me to?"

My mom sighed. "Hunter, who in the world is going to pay you to lick their head?"

Hunter shrugged. "I don't know."

"Hell, if someone would pay me, I'd lick their head," I muttered. After all, the credit card bills weren't going to pay themselves.

"Grandma paid me to file down her corns," Hunter offered.

My mom and I both shuddered at the thought of Hunter wielding an emery board on Grandma's bony old feet. "That's not the same thing. Just keep your tongue to yourself, Hunter, all right?" my mom asked. She was practically pleading at this point.

Hunter hung his head. "Okay, I guess."

"Thank you," my mom said, kissing him on his forehead.

She got in the car and started the engine, and as we drove toward our house in the dry summer heat, she said breezily, "I didn't get a chance to ask you, Ryden. How did it go?"

I shook my head mournfully. "I asked the VP if she was pregnant. Nope. She was just fat." It seemed like I was on some horrible downward spiral, with each interview somehow worse than the last. At this point I was starting to think it was something psychological—like, I didn't get the job I wanted so now I was somehow sabotaging my chances at getting any other one.

"Oh, that's unfortunate," my mom said. But then she brightened. "Well, stress does contribute to belly fat, I've heard. So that probably wouldn't be a place you'd want to work anyway. Your waistline would suffer for it. What about the other one? The interview with . . . what's that magazine? *California Locksmith?*"

"The guy asked me if I could e-mail him pictures of my feet."

"What do feet have to do with locks?" Hunter called from the backseat. He had unwrapped a leftover fruit roll-up and stuck pieces of it to his face. God, that kid was weird.

"Nothing," I told him. "That's the problem."

My mom, who had heretofore shown little interest in my job search, slapped the steering wheel and said suddenly, "You know what I'm going to do? I'm going to call Milly Freeman from high school—you know, she runs that little indie publishing house?—and I'll ask her. I'll just ask her for a favor."

I rolled down the window and stuck my head out. Maybe it'd get knocked off by a mailbox. That would be fine. "Milly's dead, Mom," I said. "Dad already called."

"Really? How terrible." Her phone rang, and after she answered it, her face went white. "Grandma? Coffin? Where?"

. . .

My paternal grandmother, Maureen Ruth McKenna Malby, lay with her hands folded on her chest, tucked inside the white satin lining of an ivory-colored casket. Soothing music, piped through invisible speakers, filled the air softly, and a bouquet of fragrant yellow roses stood nearby.

"What do you think of this one?" she said, her eyes snapping open. "Do you like it? Or do you prefer that elegant little mahogany number I was in earlier? That one had a secret compartment for valuables."

I put my face in my hands. "Grandma," I said into my palms, "I really can't think about this right now."

"Oh, yes, it's all too morbid for you?" She plucked at the satin ribbons on the casket's padded lid, and then tied two of them together in a bow.

"Yes, that's what I said." Clearly annoyed with my lack of enthusiasm for her ghoulish shopping spree, she motioned for me to get out of the way. "Come here, Hunter, what do you think of Grandma spending her eternal slumber in this one?"

Hunter shyly reached up and touched the ornate brass handle. "I love it," he breathed.

Grandma sat up and clapped her hands. "Excellent," she said to the funeral director, who had just materialized from the shadows like some kind of somberly dressed ghost. "They'll take it."

"It's an excellent choice," the man said. He had small dark eyes under heavy gray eyebrows, and he was managing, somehow, to look both solemn and enthusiastic simultaneously. What a weird job that must be, I thought. But I was desperate enough to consider asking him if he needed any help—it was only shame that stopped me. I didn't want my mom to see me begging.

"How much is it?" my mother asked, clutching her purse as if she thought he might try to run off with it.

"Eight thousand dollars," he said mildly.

"Eight *thousand* dollars?" my mother repeated, her voice an octave higher than usual.

My grandma beamed and placed her hand on the casket lid possessively.

"It's hand-carved," said the funeral director, straightening his tie.

My mom gave a distinctly unladylike cough. "By who," she said, "the pope in Rome himself?"

The funeral director smiled gently. "The carpenters who made this are monks who live and work in a small monastery in the French Alps. They are world renowned for their exquisitely wrought caskets and their organic, small-batch goat cheeses. And the casket linens are five-hundred-thread count. There's absolutely nothing softer on the skin."

Small-batch goat cheeses? I thought.

My mom glanced at my grandma, who was now pacing the display models, wanting to make sure she'd picked the nicest one. When she figured my grandma was out of earshot, she leaned forward and whispered, "Are we perhaps forgetting a key part of the equation?"

Now, Grandma sometimes feigned deafness when she wanted to ignore my dad, but the truth is her hearing is as sharp as a fox's. She was at Mom's side in a flash, her hands on her hips, squaring off with the funeral director. "That's absolutely right. Why pay all that money for a lovely coffin when there's probably a local ditch they can throw me in for free?"

"Now, now, Mom," my mother said.

"Don't Mom me," Grandma hissed. "I'm your mother-in-*law,* and you are not going to drop me out of an airplane or leave me out in the woods to be devoured by coyotes or whatever it was you were planning. I want my earthly remains cradled in five-hundred-count sheets."

"Be reasonable, Maureen," my mom began. "I'm just—"

"Five hundred!" my grandma hollered.

I figured they'd keep arguing for a while, so I wandered into the showroom where the gleaming coffins were laid out in rows, as if just waiting for dead people—or vampires, maybe—to come and fill them up. I shuddered. It was creepy, even in broad daylight.

In the corner, beneath a spray of lilies, lay a long blue

casket with lightning-bolt decals around the edges. It was set off from the other caskets, and it was the only one in the room with a closed lid.

Is that the San Diego Chargers theme on it? I wondered. Someone would have to be a really big fan, that was certain. Which made me stop and think: if one's coffin should symbolize one's life, what would I be buried in? A coffin that looked like a book? Or maybe one like a big red editing pencil? I grinned ruefully to myself: judging by the recent weeks, my coffin would more likely look like a giant unemployment check.

I crept toward the Chargers coffin, its closed lid almost convincing me that there was a dead body in it. I touched one of the lightning bolts, noticing how the handles of the coffin seemed to be made out of pigskin, just like a football.

Ewww, I thought. Who knew something so tacky could be so chilling?

That was when the lid flung open.

My heart skipped a beat—hell, it skipped about twenty of them. Hunter sat up, and screamed, "Boo!" I stumbled backward, clutching my chest, already informing Hunter, at the top of my lungs, that I was going to cream his sorry little ass just as soon as I could breathe again.

And maybe I would have, or maybe I would have laughed it off. But I never got to test the limits of my forgiveness, because my backward motion sent me barreling into a different coffin, just as the funeral director, my mother, and my grandma came rushing over to see what all the commotion was about.

I reached for the teetering box, my fingers sliding across its lacquered surface. "Oh, dear God, no," I gasped, as I felt the giant weight of it tipping away from me. The funeral director lunged for it, too, but he was too late, and we stood there dumbfounded as the entire thing went crashing to the floor.

Shitshitshitshit.

"Oh, Christ." My mother sighed.

"You break, you buy!" Hunter said brightly, pointing to a sign saying the very same thing.

Remember how I said that if you ever wanted to be stared at, you should try running down an L.A. sidewalk in stilettos and a pencil skirt on your way to an interview? Scratch that. If you ever *truly* want to be stared at, try driving down Wilshire Boulevard in your mother's pink Le Baron with an enormous, half-shattered coffin strapped to the roof. Everyone and his brother—not to mention his uncle, his sister, his second-cousin-once-removed, his therapist, and his yoga teacher—will stare at you. And you have no idea how freaky that makes a girl feel.

CHAPTER 11

"Look at how her fingers are positioned," Adam said, pointing. "See? She's playing a C chord."

Obediently I gazed at the slim, painted fingers of the doe-eyed woman in *Lady Playing a Lute*. "Is that supposed to inspire me?" I asked. "Because you *know* how hopeless I am, which means you should also know that staring at a picture that some dude painted in the sixteenth century is not going to help me remember which fingers go on which string. Plus, she's playing a lute, not a guitar. See? It says so right on the plaque."

Adam and I had decided to take a break from our usual activities—which for me meant a day I didn't have to wear that damn pencil skirt and smile ingratiatingly to a person who had no interest in hiring me, and for him meant a day in which he didn't lie around the house, noodling on his guitar and trying to decide whether or not to go to law school—in order to come to the Getty Museum. We'd wandered through the hushed white halls and gazed up at drawings of gods and demons, and at paintings of pastoral landscapes and bloody battles.

Adam leaned in to read the plaque. "It also says they used to think that Leonardo da Vinci painted this. Wouldn't that be a bummer, to think you'd bought a da Vinci and then find out it was just this Bartolomeo Veneto guy?"

I nodded. "Way worse than buying a book you thought was by the teenaged son of a truck-stop prostitute and later finding out it was written by a middle-aged woman."

Adam looked at me blankly.

"Hello," I said. "The whole T. J. Sanders story? How he supposedly wrote these books but there was really no such person? Were you living under a log? It was on *Oprah* and everything. Trust me, it was a big scandal."

Adam gazed contemplatively at the lady and her lute. "Missed it," he said, clearly not caring that he had.

Which was actually good, I thought. If we went to the same school, hung out all the time, always agreed on which animals we'd rather be, *and* knew all the same stuff, both musical and literary, we might as well be the same person. And it would be hard to be best friends with yourself.

We went outside, bought two overpriced waters from the refreshment stand, and walked down into the gardens to the spot where you can look out over the whole city. The sky was blue, but a gray-brown haze hovered over the downtown buildings, making them seem faint and blurry.

"I'd miss it here if I left," Adam mused, staring out at the buildings. "And my lungs would probably go into shock from lack of smog."

I leaned against the cool stone wall and squinted into the distance. "Well, New York has its share of fumes, I'm sure. It's not like Columbia is in the middle of an old-growth forest or something."

"True," Adam acknowledged. "And if I ever felt like the air was too clean I could just put my nose up to a taxi's tailpipe and breathe in."

"Exactly. Or you could camp out in Times Square with that Naked Cowboy. That would help you get your daily allotment of carbon monoxide." I turned to him, suddenly feeling more serious. "Not like I think you should go, though." I paused. "I mean, if you want to and everything. But . . ." I stopped, uncertain of what I wanted to say.

Adam peered over the wall and down the canyon. "Oh,

let's not talk about this boring stuff. You know I like to avoid serious conversations whenever possible. We're at the museum! Let's talk about art."

I watched as an elderly couple strolled past us, hand in hand, peering at the map of the gardens. They looked happy, if somewhat lost, and I felt a weird surge of good will toward them. "Okay, what art do you want to talk about?"

He thought about this for a while. "Um, have you seen the commercial for the Getty? The one where people are walking around L.A., but instead of heads they've got paintings? Or, like, plants from the garden?"

I laughed. "That doesn't count as talking about art. That's talking about the marketing of art."

"What can I say?" Adam shrugged. "I'm just a stupid rock musician."

"True," I said, sighing. "Meanwhile I am a paragon of higher culture."

"Is that why no magazine in all of Los Angeles wants to hire you? You're just too sophisticated?" He crossed his arms and grinned at me.

I punched him. "Not fair," I said. "Don't kick a girl when she's down."

"Ow," Adam said, rubbing where I'd hit him. "Sorry. Jeez, it was just a joke. But hey, I know what'll make you feel better. How about a delicious, chocolaty Esk—"

I had already started walking toward the exit. "Screw the Eskimo Pie," I said, turning back to look at him. "Let's get a drink."

I was lounging on the front lawn, working on my tan—because, as my dad had unhelpfully pointed out, I wasn't working on anything else, and without my car, I had no way of getting anywhere anyway—when a big, 1980s-style van with copper paint and gold trim came racing up the street and squealed to a stop right in front of our house. Out of the driver's side door tumbled a heavyset middle-aged guy in Ray-Bans with black hair that looked like an otter pelt on his head. I watched somewhat apprehensively as he walked up the driveway toward me.

Apparently he was a fan of red bikinis, because he gave me a lecherous smile and seemed to search around for a conversation starter (other than "I can rub that Coppertone on you" or something, which I was willing to bet was his general style of opener). But then his eyes fell upon the half-shattered hulk of the purple coffin, which was also on our front lawn—did I mention it was the exact color of Barney, the purple dinosaur?—and the smile quickly vanished.

"Can I help you?" I asked, covering myself up with my towel.

He tore his gaze away from the coffin and cleared his throat. "I'm looking for—"

"Gary," my father bellowed, striding out of the house wearing a T-shirt that said WHERE'S YOUR ASPEN? (Ha ha, get it? As in: WHERE'S YOUR ASS BEEN? Talk about a paragon of higher culture.) "You're late!" he said. He held out his hand and grasped Gary's in a firm handshake. "Where's the stuff?"

Gary turned and pointed to his van. "All in there," he said.

"Well, bring them out!" my dad exclaimed. "Let's see those babies!"

He kicked a broken fragment of the coffin aside impatiently. Why he hadn't bothered to put the thing in the garage I'd never know. I mean, what was he planning on doing with it? Maybe he was hoping to intimidate our hot Brazilian neighbor. Like, *if your cat shits on my driveway again it's going to end up in a box*. But it was more likely that he just hadn't gotten around to moving it since he was so busy planning his awesome new Internet business.

Gary lumbered down to the van and returned with a large cardboard box, which my dad eagerly peered into. He reached in and pulled out a large, gleaming belt buckle. I couldn't see what was on it from my position on the lawn, but I was willing to bet it was a fish or a cougar or something similarly manly. "Interesting craftsmanship," my dad mused. "Tasteful design."

Oh, dear, I thought. Because if my dad thought it was

tasteful, it was pretty much guaranteed to be awful. And what was worse, he was passionate about his aesthetics. While most men, aware that they have questionable style, leave things like home décor and accessory purchasing to their wives, my dad did not. He took charge. Which was why there was one year when our house was full of macramé owls, and another when it was impossible to walk into any room without stepping on a Turkish carpet or a brightly colored silk pillow.

"Yes," my dad murmured. "Very interesting."

"If you like," Gary said, "I can get you many more. These are valuable things!"

As my dad inspected the buckle, turning it this way and that, Hunter materialized out of a rhododendron bush and crept toward him over the grass. He was dressed in a long black cape and sporting very sharp-looking plastic canines. He held his finger up to his lips, indicating I should be quiet. He had a trickle of fake blood running down his chin.

My dad, absorbed in his careful perusal of the buckle shipment, did not notice Hunter until he leaped forward with a high-pitched shriek.

"I'm Hugo the vampire!" Hunter cried, inserting himself between Dad and greasy Gary and waving his arms around madly.

"Jesus Christ," my dad yelled, grasping at his heart.

"I vant to suck your blood, Valter!" Hunter squinted his red-lined eyes up at my dad and said menacingly, "I am hungry for the blood of a fat man!"

After my dad realized he was not in fact having a heart attack, he smiled at Hunter, though it was through gritted teeth. "Now is not the time, *Hugo*. For one thing, your father is not fat. For another, I am doing business here."

Undeterred, Hunter hopped from foot to foot. "Suck your blood, suck your blood," he chanted.

"Hugo . . ." my dad warned.

My brother stopped dancing and looked up at Dad. "Help me build my boxcar," he said. "I want to win the race. It's in like, a month. And all the other kids have already started theirs. Jimmy Gill says his dad is—"

"I said I'm doing business," my dad interrupted.

With a theatrical sigh, my brother the grade-school vampire scuttled off, probably to go suck the cream filling out of a Twinkie, which was, when it came down to it, much more his style. I mean, really, the kid couldn't even stand the *sight* of blood. The last time he cut himself (with a pair of Grandma's sewing shears) he fainted on the bathroom floor.

I watched with consternation as my dad pulled an envelope, thick with cash, from his back pocket, and accepted the box from Gary, who pocketed it with greedy enthusiasm. The two men shook hands again, and then Gary slinked back to his van and peeled away, leaving two black skid marks on our street.

"Ryden, come here!" my dad said gleefully. "Check this out!"

Dutifully obeying him, though not without a certain amount of dread in my heart, I walked over and peered into the box to see hundreds of big, shiny, and highly tacky belt buckles. "Wow," I said. "Those are really . . . really . . . really something, Dad."

"My first order." He held up a buckle shaped like a wolf. It was so big it could have been Mel Gibson's shield in *Braveheart*.

"So," he said. "Would you, as vice president, like to spearhead the marketing effort?"

I nearly choked on the water I was sipping. "Marketing effort?"

My dad nodded enthusiastically. "You know, ads, slogans, tag lines. You could give each buckle a flashy name. Like"—and here he held up one with a snake on it—"the Viper. Or"—he reached for another one—"the State of Delaware."

I took Delaware from him. "Wow. I hardly know what to say."

He dangled a buckle shaped like a can of Coors in front of my face. "Come on, I need your input. You're young. You know what's in style."

I tried to make my voice gentle when I said, "That's so nice of you to want to include me, but no, thank you. I couldn't."

"I'll make us business cards on the laser printer?" he offered.

Now I was just getting annoyed. What was his *problem*? This was a man who'd convinced himself that he could single-handedly revive the Pet Rock craze, which was why we still had a mountain of stones in our backyard. A year later he'd decided that boomerangs with neon flashing lights were the toy of the future. (And then, when faced with the predictable surplus of those ridiculous objects, he'd started sending them to our relatives at Christmas, a gift even more unwelcome than my mom's fruitcake.) And don't get me started on the ferrets.

I grabbed the Coors buckle and tossed it down into the box. "You know what I want as *vice president,* Dad? I want my car back. I want to stop riding a bus, calling a taxi, or being ferried around in a Le Baron with a coffin on the roof every time I need to leave the house."

"I told you, I'm waiting for a part from the factory," my dad said, picking up the buckle and checking to make sure I hadn't nicked it.

I just didn't want to hear it anymore. "Maybe you should take your buckles inside," I said, "and start thinking about some catchy slogans. Like 'Need a chuckle? Buy an ugly belt buckle.' Or 'Want to hide your belly fat? A big steel buckle is where it's at!'"

My dad looked vaguely insulted. But he was not so easy to discourage. "You could use a real attitude adjustment, kiddo. Now why don't we take this box up to your room and see if we can't find a place for it."

"*My* room? Why my room?" There was hardly a spare inch in it, thanks to all his junk. I couldn't tell you the number of times I'd woken up with one of those little medieval warriors stuck to my cheek.

My dad looked at me as if this were an incredibly stupid question. "Because it was supposed to be *my* room now, because you were supposed to leave home. But you haven't, as you may have noticed. And I figure as long as you're here, you might as well help out a little. You're not the only one with bills to pay, you know. Your mother's been going a little crazy at Wal-Mart lately—I think it's a coping mechanism because Hunter's such a goddamn weirdo—and now Grandma's going to have to spend eternity in a cardboard box thanks to you."

I threw up my hands. "I told you, it was an accident! I said I was sorry. What do you want me to do?"

My dad waggled his finger in my face. "I want you to get off your bum and start pulling some weight around here."

"Agh!" I howled, kicking at the box of buckles. "That's

so unfair. I'm scouring the job market. I wake up every morning and go on Craigslist searching for some new gem of a job. Do you have any *clue* what these interviews are like? Am I a team player? Can I multitask? Is my hand-shake too firm? Is my posture crap? Can they tell I'm sweating profusely because I just rode to this interview on a Schwinn bicycle? Do I have pretty feet, and if so, do I want to e-mail pictures of them? The last thing I need from you right now is a speech about how I'm not pulling my own weight. I am freaking *trying* here. I was just taking a lunch break."

His expression softened, and it seemed like maybe he even felt a little sorry for me. He lifted up the box, groan-ing under the weight, and said mildly, "Well, maybe you're setting your sights too high."

I was still annoyed, though. "Oh, really? And where do you think I should set my sights?"

He raised his eyebrows, looking thoughtful, and then a smile spread across his face as he headed back toward the house.

CHAPTER 12

"Welcome to Luggage World," I grumbled to the elderly couple who'd just hobbled through the door. "Can I help you find something?"

"Some luggage," the old woman said, baring big, white, and obviously false teeth. "You can help us find some luggage. That is what you sell here, isn't it?"

"Be nice, Frances," the old man told her. "Can't you see how miserable this pretty little girl is?" He tipped his golf cap at me and then gestured to his wife. "She woke up on the wrong side of the waterbed this morning, poor dear."

"'Sokay," I muttered. The old man was right: I was

miserable. I'd left college with dreams of fascinating jobs and fat paychecks, and here I was, the new sales associate at Luggage World, wearing a polyester bellhop uniform and chafing under the watchful eyes of my father, Walter Malby, Regional Manager and Suitcase Salesman Extraordinaire. I had tried to think of other, more humiliating moments in my life—the time my bikini top fell off when I was bouncing on the end of a diving board; the day I walked around with two mismatched boots and no one bothered to tell me; the party where I got really drunk and made out with a hairy frat guy who called himself Dr. Sloppy. I didn't think that any of them compared to this.

I led the couple over to a mound of flowered bags. "These are all on clearance." The old woman began to fiddle with the zippers, sucking all the while on her false teeth.

"What they lack in style they make up for in price," I offered. These old folks knew the game, so I didn't even try to sound cheerful.

I was watching the old man try to figure out how to work the extension handle on the biggest of the suitcases when my dad came out of nowhere and grabbed my elbow, pulling me into the Samsonite aisle.

He put his face right up in front of mine and said, "Your customer service skills are shit. Your eye contact is nonexistent and your posture is terrible." Then he stepped back and gave me an appraising once-over. "And you look like someone just took a dump in your lunchbox," he pronounced.

I pulled off my hat and held it out to him so that he could see the scratchy inner lining that had been torturing me all morning. "Do you have any idea how uncomfortable this uniform is? It's so synthetic I feel like I'm walking around in some giant rubber glove. I want to be wearing a Diane von Furstenberg wrap dress and the perfect pair of boots, not some polyester flunky costume with loafers I borrowed from Mom."

My dad drew himself up stiffly. "I'll ask you to remember that I wore that uniform for ten years, young lady, and it's what put the Tater Tots on your dinner plate." Then he put his hand on my shoulder. "Look," he said, more kindly. "It's the positive attitude that makes the sale. Now watch how it's done. You be the customer." He plastered a huge, happy smile on his face and clapped his hands together. "Hey, how are you today?" he asked me. "Going out of town, huh?"

Reluctantly I played along. "Uh, yeah."

"And where are you heading, might I ask?" my dad said, still grinning. I'd never heard him sound so friendly in his life, and it freaked me out a little.

"Maui?" I said.

Dad clapped his hands again in delight. "Maui! Wonderful! Business or pleasure?"

"Um, business?" I was bored of this game already.

"No!" my dad hissed, his nice-salesman voice gone instantly. "Nobody goes to Maui for business. Just say pleasure."

"Then why did you ask me the question?"

He pulled a big blue Samsonite off the shelf and plopped it on the floor in front of me. "Just watch my salesmanship, okay?" He pointed at the suitcase with a flourish. "Isn't this amazing? Its wheels are so smooth it can roll down airport hallways forever. It's got a dual suspension axle and special brake action for when you need to stop quickly to get yourself a Starbucks." He unzipped it with effortless flair. "And look, inside there's a secret pocket for all your valuables." He paused, and then reverted back to Dad the dad. "If you get any valuables, that is. May I remind you that you work on commission?" The doorbell chimed then, and he smiled brightly. "Now you go get 'em, tiger," he said. "I'll take care of the geriatrics here. They only want the cheap crap anyway."

"Okay." I sighed. I tried to stand tall as I walked toward the door. A woman stood with her back to me, talking on a cell phone. When I heard her say good-bye, I made my voice as cheerful as possible and said, "Hi! Going out of town?"

The woman spun around, snapping her cell phone shut, and when I saw her face I suddenly wished I had been hit by a bus on the way to work. Jessica Bard, the lovely, ass-kissy, striving Jessica Bard, had just walked into Luggage World, and she was looking at me with an expression of deep surprise. She was wearing an unbearably chic little black suit with a chunky gold necklace and strappy yellow heels.

"Oh, hi!" Jessica said brightly. "Ryden! I didn't know you . . . worked here." She gave a dubious look around the store, and I saw it through her cool blue eyes: the faded carpet, the garish signs proclaiming 30% OFF THE LUXE LINE BY BORDEN and FREE LAYAWAY, and the harsh fluorescent light that made us all look twice our age.

I glanced back toward the old couple, desperate for an escape. But my dad was helping them choose a hideous lavender carry-on, which meant I had no obvious excuse to run away. So I turned back to Jessica. "I don't," I said. "I mean, not really. It's just temporary. I'm just helping out my dad."

"Okay," Jessica said. "Well, that's nice of you."

I couldn't tell if she was being sincere or not, but I forced myself to give her the benefit of the doubt. "So, uh, how's Happerman and Browning?" I asked, though I most definitely did not want to hear the answer.

Jessica's face lit up. "Incredible. Really great. They're sending me to New York for a conference next week. Hence the need for a new suitcase. I mean, my old one is a little worse for the wear since the Thailand trip. A ticket to Phuket was my graduation present from my parents."

I tried to keep a positive expression. "Sounds awesome." *I hope you picked up some intestinal parasite there,* I thought. *Or maybe some horrible tapeworm.*

"Yeah. And it was so cool of Happerman and Browning to let me go. I'd only worked there two weeks before I went off for a two-week vacation. Anyway, can I see that black one?"

I grabbed a step stool and reached up to grab the one she was pointing to. After Jessica poked at it for a few minutes she said, "How about that gray one over there?" She gestured toward the other side of the store.

I hoisted up the stool and marched across the store, Jessica daintily following me in her heels. Fabulous trips, wonderful jobs: I *so* did not want to hear anything else she had to say.

"I mean, it's a really intense position," she said to my back. "Like for the first time in my life I actually feel challenged, you know?"

"You mean you can't buy Snaff off with a batch of muffins?" I muttered.

"Sometimes I wish they'd hired more than one assistant editor. Like you, for instance. It would have been nice to work with you. You could have helped me deal with Jonathan Micah Miller, who has a new book coming out and who is not as nice as he likes to pretend. I mean, I think you and I have synergy. Remember when we did that project together in freshman English—that paper on Dante's *Inferno*?"

"Yeah," I said, reaching for the gray suitcase. I remembered our paper—we titled it "Putting the Hell in Hello: Dante's Conversations with the Fallen Angels." And I was pretty sure I was deep in some circle of Hell right now. "Synergy, yeah, whatever you say."

"Seriously, this could really work. I mean, they're working me pretty hard," Jessica said, turning over the price tag and raising her eyebrows. "Three hundred? Must be a really special suitcase. But anyway, I know things are tough right now for you—I mean, look at that outfit you're wearing; you look like a valet or something—but you have to remember: 'Struggle and strife come before success. Even in the dictionary.'" She smiled brightly at me.

That was it. That was all I could take. I ripped off my horrible itchy hat and threw it on the floor, and then I flung off my polyester jacket, too. "Dad," I hollered.

"You've got a customer!" And then I stormed out of Luggage World.

As I stomped my way to the bus stop, feeling the July sun beating down on my face, I told myself that I'd rather sell my body on Hollywood Boulevard than peddle suitcases to senior citizens and corporate suck-ups. Jessica Bard! I hoped she would take a big bite of one of her homemade muffins and then choke on it.

I moved aside an old newspaper and sat down on the bench to wait for the Number 20 bus. I could feel my skin burning, but there was no shade in sight. It just wasn't fair, I thought. New York? New suitcases? Jessica Bard had everything going for her. For all I knew she'd moved into the Beautiful Loft Apartment within walking distance of Happerman & Browning and every night she sipped a glass of Chardonnay on her balcony and congratulated herself on how great she was. As far as I knew, the only thing she'd ever tried for and failed to get was Adam. She'd had a crush on him our sophomore year, and though they'd gone on a few dates, Adam had never been interested.

My phone beeped with a text.

Moth or snail? it read.

Speak of the devil. And the question was an easy one. I typed: *Snail. Snails have own houses. Don't have to live with parents.*

Squirrel or rat?

Another easy one, though counterintuitive perhaps. *Rats don't rely on handouts. They are tough bastards.*

Chicken or duck?

I sighed. The next bus wasn't due for forty minutes, so I might as well keep playing. *Chicken. At least a chicken has a goddamn job.*

Huh?

It lays eggs! I texted.

My phone rang then, and of course it was Adam. (Every once in a while his famous patience failed him during our texting exchanges, because I was a notoriously slow typist.) "Ducks lay eggs, too, you know," he said. "But you're right, not on the scale that the chicken does. Why did the chicken cross the road?"

"To drown himself in the pond on the other side?" I said glumly.

Adam pressed one of the keys on the phone so it beeped loudly in my ear. He did that every time I annoyed him. "Because he wanted to, goddammit. That's the goddamn reason."

Another stray newspaper blew across the sidewalk toward me and then wrapped itself around my ankle. Gross. "You sound like my dad or something," I said, kicking it off.

"Very perceptive," Adam said. "I was, in fact, just doing my impression of him. What did you think?"

I laughed halfheartedly. "Huh. Well, you may not want to go to law school, but don't go into comedy, all right? I don't think you're ready."

"I think I'm extremely funny," Adam said, and then blew a single note on his harmonica. "Anyway, that's not why I called. I wanted to remind you about that party tomorrow night," he said. "For Bastille Day. It'll definitely cheer you up."

A man wearing nothing but spandex leggings sat down beside me on the bench and proceeded to examine his chest hairs one by one. I scooted as far away from him as I could. "Well, it can't make me feel worse," I said.

But as anyone with half a brain knows, of course it could.

CHAPTER 13

My Escort was still being "fixed" by my dad. And by fixed
I mean "stared at" and "poked at with inappropriate tools."
I tried not to mourn it too much—I told myself there was
a better car in my future. Needless to say, Adam was my
ride to the party.

"I'm starving," Adam said as we pulled out of my driveway. He was wearing a sweater draped over his shoulders
and he looked very preppy. But he could pull it off. "Are
you starving?"

"Always," I said, rolling down the window. His car
didn't have AC, but who was I to complain? "Food is my
only comfort these days."

He told me to stop being so melodramatic and pointed us toward his favorite taco stand, an aluminum trailer off Ventura, somewhere in Studio City. He'd been going there ever since he got his license, and by now he was friends with the proprietors. He played basketball with their son in the afternoons.

"Adam Davies!" called the middle-aged man in the stained apron as he wiped a picnic table clean. "We haven't seen you for a while."

"Hey, Luis," Adam said, striding up and shaking his hand. "Good to see you. How's Benetta? How's Julio? I'm dying for tacos."

Luis smiled and ducked into his modified Airstream. "Couldn't be better. Who's your pretty friend?"

Adam put his arm around me. "This is Ryden. We've been friends forever but you've never met her because until about a month ago she didn't like Mexican food. How crazy is that? But finally, after years of encouragement, I got her to like tacos. And suddenly she was all over the mole, the enchiladas, everything."

Luis laughed. "A convert! My favorite." He busied himself at the grill and, in short order, handed us four fish tacos, the smell of which made my mouth water.

Adam paid and we sat on the picnic table bench and watched the cars go by as we ate. It was true what Adam said—I used to hate Mexican food, which made me feel like a fake Californian. Now, though, I loved it, and pozole was my favorite. I could eat that stuff all day long.

"So you quit Luggage World," he said, picking up a stray shred of cabbage and popping it into his mouth. "You just bagged on it." He paused. "Get it? 'Bagged'?"

"You're hilarious," I said as I bit into my taco.

"Hey, no one ever said I was going to quit my day job."

I shot him a look. "May I remind you that you don't *have* a day job?"

Adam grinned. "Oh, right. I just lie around all day trying to figure out whether to be a lawyer or a rock star."

I squirted a big stream of hot sauce onto my taco. "While I lie around contemplating whether to apply to the Shell station down the street or start standing on the street corner with a sign that says WILL WORK FOR WORK."

Adam rolled his eyes. "Can't we talk about something else?" he asked. "Look at this whole big world and all the things there are to talk about in it."

"Like what?"

He thought for a moment. "I don't know."

"See?" I said, poking him in the arm. "There *are* no other subjects."

"Oh, I know," he exclaimed. "Which would you rather

be, a shark or a whale?" He stuffed the last of the taco in his mouth and looked at me expectantly.

"I could really care less," I said. "Let's go."

In the darkening evening, the hulking stucco McMansion surrounded by a high wall looked more like a boutique prison than a good place to have a summer party.

"They've even got iron bars on the windows," I pointed out to Adam as we approached.

"Those are merely decorative," he said. "It's the old Mission style. Anyway, it's fitting for the day, isn't it? I mean, we are celebrating the storming of the Bastille. The freedom of the French prisoners."

"We're celebrating the fact that yesterday I had a job for all of two hours," I said, straightening my skirt. I hoped it wasn't too short, but I'd been eager to show off my tan. After all, what else did I have to show for the last month? "I made fifteen dollars, before taxes. Whose party is this again?"

Adam handed me a beer from the six-pack we'd brought, though we weren't even inside yet. "Martin Black's." He said this as if I ought to know who that was.

"Who?"

"He lived on our hall sophomore year. His parents are shrinks and he was an anthropology major."

I conjured up a faint memory of a skinny kid with

wild curly hair and a spasmodic way of dancing. "The guy who used to dance like he was having a seizure?"

Adam nodded. "The last time I saw him it was all I could do not to run and put my wallet between his teeth so he didn't bite his tongue off."

"Okay, I know who you're talking about then." Martin had always struck me as kind of a loser, but he obviously knew a lot of people. We'd had to park six blocks away.

"Didn't he used to say that eating sushi naked was the most erotic thing in the world?" I asked.

Adam nodded. "Yep."

"See, I don't understand that," I said, opening my beer with a flourish. "It makes sense to eat pomegranates naked, for example, because the juice squirts everywhere and it totally stains. But salmon skin rolls? I don't see the point."

Adam laughed. "People have strange ideas about what's erotic. I knew a guy who liked to watch girls take off their shoes and then walk around in big pans of refried beans."

I turned and stared at him. "You're kidding me, right?"

Adam shrugged. "Hey, to each his own. Fetishes are generally harmless."

I decided to let the matter drop before he started telling me about someone in our Shakespeare class who was a total Plushie or something. I mean, there were some things you just didn't want to know about a person, like whether or not they found stuffed animals sexually attractive.

We walked up to the imposing front door. There were two large stone lions guarding either side, one of which was wearing a Dodgers baseball cap, while the other had a cigarette taped to its mouth. "Classy," Adam said, turning the lion's cap sideways. "There you go, buddy. Now you look fly." He approached the other lion, looking thoughtful. "But *you* need something besides a cigarette. That's such a nasty habit. What would your mother say?" He reached up, plucked a lovely pink rose from one of the lushly blossoming bushes nearby, and tucked it between the lion's front paws. "Much better."

"Hey, Dr. Doolittle," I said, taking a swig of my beer, "are we going in or what?"

Adam tweaked the position of the rose just slightly, and then straightened up and held out his arm. I put my hand in the crook of his elbow, and together we entered the large and gaudy home of the boy who loved to eat raw fish naked.

In the vast sunken living room, I spotted various college acquaintances-slash-Facebook friends lounging on the leather couches, drinking margaritas. I waved to Ken from my econ lecture (the one class I almost failed) and Julie from our Shakespeare and the Theater of Consciousness seminar, but I didn't want to talk to them. I hung back by Adam, who had finished his first beer already and was moving on to his second.

That mashup of "Gold Digger" and Beethoven's Fifth was playing on the stereo, and Christmas lights had been strung up on the walls. A coed in a skirt so short it really should have been a belt wandered by, giving Adam the once-over before moving on.

"Did that girl just check me out?" Adam asked, looking pleased.

I nodded and picked a piece of lint off his shirt. "But don't get a big head or anything. I mean, you've got dryer lint on you."

He looked down and picked off another piece. "No worries on the big head thing. I am by nature both modest and self-effacing." He handed me another beer, even though I wasn't done with mine. "In addition to being extremely handsome."

"Oh, shut up," I said. But out of the corner of my eye I took him in. He really was handsome, though after all these years it was hard for me to see it. Other people looked at him and saw a tall guy with thick sandy hair and long-lashed green eyes, high cheekbones, and a good, straight nose. When I looked at him I usually saw what he'd been: a skinny, slightly goofy-looking boy in knee socks and polyester athletic shorts, banging on the keys of our basement piano or sitting at our kitchen table gorging himself on the Cookie Crisp cereal I'd begged my mom to buy me for getting a check-plus in penmanship on my fifth-grade report card.

"I think I'm going to need something stronger if I'm going to enjoy this party," Adam said. "Want to find the real booze?"

I glanced around at the motley crowd eating chips and making half-drunk small talk. It was just so . . . so *college*. And weren't we supposed to be beyond that? "Definitely."

We pushed our way through the crowd and found ourselves on the back deck, where a tiki bar strung with lights shaped like chili peppers offered us our choice of gleaming bottles.

"Would you rather be a scotch or a gin?" Adam asked, holding up a handle of each.

I scratched my chin thoughtfully. "Gin," I said. "With a side of tonic."

"A fine choice. Coming right up."

I stared out into the crowd while he fixed us our drinks, watching a group of people I seemed to vaguely recall from my psych seminar pass around a bottle of SoCo. But I was brought quickly and unpleasantly back to attention by Jessica Bard's unmistakable chirp coming from over by the pool. "So they keep calling me," she was saying, "because they've got my résumé and everything, but I'm already working at Happerman, and so I'm like, make me a better offer and we'll talk, you know?"

"Hey, you've got to play hardball," some blond dude in a V-neck T-shirt agreed. "That's the name of the game these days. You've got to be your own free agent."

"That's just what I'm saying," Jessica exclaimed.

They were heading for the tiki bar, and I looked wildly around for any place to hide. There was a large rhododendron just a few feet away. *What the hell,* I thought, and sprang toward it. Unfortunately, that's when Jessica saw me. Her face brightened. "Ryden! Fancy seeing you again so soon! Small world, isn't it?"

"I guess," I allowed, extracting myself from the outer edges of the bush. If only I'd been just a little bit faster, I'd have been safe and invisible, deep in its shiny green leaves!

"Hey, man," the V-necked blond dude said, coming up to Adam. "I haven't seen you since poli-sci. What are you up to?"

Adam raised his glass. "Just getting a buzz on, buddy."

I stifled a small chuckle. Adam never used the word "buddy" unless he really couldn't stand a person.

"I'm Andy," the blond said, sticking his hand out to shake mine. "And this here is Ted and that's Maureen." He pointed to two friends who had come up behind him,

Coronas in hand. "Ted and I are at Global Finance to-gether. We're going to see who gets the corner office first, right, man?" Here Andy lobbed a fake punch at Ted, who grinned and ducked.

"And it's going to be me, sucker," Ted said. "You don't have the nads for high-risk bets." He lowered his sun-glasses over his eyes, even though it was dark, and tried to look appropriately macho.

"They think they're so cool," Maureen said, helping herself to a plate of pineapple slices. "Just because they're in finance. Well, I happen to think that going to med school is a pretty cool thing, too."

Adam tried to feign interest. He was by nature polite. "Med school, huh?"

"Johns Hopkins," Maureen confirmed, trying (and failing) not to look too proud of herself. "My roommate Heather is going to Yale."

I poured more gin into my drink and sloshed a bit of tonic in, just for show. Who were these people, and why were we supposed to care what they were doing with their lives? That's what I wanted to know.

"And what about you?" Andy asked, pointing to me. "What are you doing with your pretty self?"

I should have known my turn was coming. I should have kept on walking right into that rhododendron, no matter how weird it looked. Clearly I was not thinking straight; otherwise I'd already be halfway back to my parents' house, already anticipating a big bowl of popcorn and a TV turned to the CW. "Um, I'm sort of in between things right now," I said. "I'm just searching for . . . for the best opportunity, really." No one said anything, so I felt compelled to go on. "I mean, I've met some really interesting people in my interviews. Lots of interesting work out there . . . Yeah . . ."

"You're not at Luggage World anymore?" Jessica asked innocently.

"I was just helping out my dad for the day," I said. "That's not my real job."

"Well, you looked really cute in that uniform," Jessica said. "Not many people could pull off polyester and brass buttons like that, but you did."

I gazed up at the midnight-blue sky, hoping some alien ship would appear and beam me up into its silvery hold. They could prod me with their Martian instruments for an entire week and it wouldn't be half as bad as this.

"Sounds to me like you don't have a real job," Andy pointed out.

"She's a trust fund brat," Adam interjected, and then dragged me away toward the pool.

We stood in the shadows, our faces only faintly lit by a rope of Christmas lights nearby. I hung my head in shame. "God, that was so mortifying."

Adam kept his hand around my wrist and gave it a little squeeze. "Well, they may know you're unemployed, but at least they think you're rich." He grinned.

I gazed up at him mournfully. "Am I really so pitiful that you have to cover for me?"

"Do you want the real answer?" he asked.

"No."

He let my wrist go and put his arm around my shoulders. I leaned against him and smelled the homey scent of fabric softener.

"Ryden, you're not pitiful at all," he said gently.

"But I feel like such a loser! Everyone is doing something with their lives, and I'm just doing nothing but failing at everything."

"You're not a loser," he insisted. "You're just incompetent."

I stared at him.

"I'm kidding!" he said. He stepped away from me and motioned me to follow. "Come here."

I stood my ground. "I don't want another little pity hug."

He patted his broad chest. "Come on, you poor, pathetic, little no-talent screwup."

"Go ahead, joke! You got into law school!"

He laughed. "Yeah, so?"

"It means you're good, you're set, whatever. You can

put on a tie every morning and go in to work, and you can have your secretary make your lunch dates, and you can play squash at six with your friend from the office and then hit happy hour at Señor Swanky's and date some hot paralegal named Marigold."

"Marigold?" Adam asked. "Señor Swanky's?"

"Yes," I cried. "They have a good happy hour, I read about it in *Time Out New York* when I was at the dentist's. And Marigold will be blond and have big boobs. She'll have legs and she'll know how to use them."

Adam took a step back. "Whoa—have you always been this jealous of Marigold?"

I sighed and picked at the string of lights. "I don't know. I'm just so confused."

"Look, maybe I'm 'set,' as you say," he said gently. "But that doesn't mean I'm going to be happy." He stepped out onto the diving board, which bounced lightly under his weight. "Come here."

I stood my ground. "Screw you. I'm not going up there so you can push me in."

"Who said anything about going in? Just come here so I can tell you something." He held his arms out again.

I glanced at the board, which was already bending down toward the water. "I don't think it looks very sturdy."

"Quit bitching and come on. When have I led you astray?"

I thought about that for a minute. "When you dared me to eat two chicken burritos and then made me go on the Ferris wheel."

"Touché," he said, a smile spreading across his face at the memory. "But really. Come here."

So I gave in. I took off my heels and stepped out onto the board, which felt even more precarious than I'd expected. "So what do you want to tell me?"

"You're not out far enough. You have to come closer."

"I will totally kill you twice over if you throw me in," I said, tiptoeing toward him. "And I already have the coffin to bury you in." When I was right in front of him I put my hands on my hips and said, "So tell me already."

He smiled a big, goofy smile. "I'm opening at Mint next Thursday."

I let out a shriek. "Shut up! Are you kidding me? That's amazing. Screw law school, you're going to be a world-famous musician! Why didn't you tell me earlier?"

Adam held his finger to his lips. "Calm down, little pony. I'm not saying no to law school necessarily."

"So you're going to Columbia, then."

Adam stared out over the water, looking somewhat annoyed. "I'm not saying that, either."

"So what are you saying? And don't give me the shrug."

Adam threw up his hands. "I'm saying I don't know what I'm going to do, Ryden! I. Don't. Know. You have the hard part figured out. You know what you want. Just stop being in such a rush to get it. Things will work out. Drink your damn gin and try to enjoy yourself. I mean, we're at a party in L.A. in the summertime. On Bastille Day. There's a guy over there with a beret and a hunk of Brie, and he's ready to wish all of us a *bonsoir.* What more do you want?"

I looked where Adam was pointing. And sure enough, there was a guy wearing a beret and dancing with a wheel of Brie to "ABC" by the Jackson 5. Where did Martin find these people?

"I want a job so I don't have to become an understudy to Buckles the Begging Clown," I said, but my voice was muffled in Adam's chest as he pulled me toward him and wrapped his arms tightly around my shoulders.

CHAPTER 14

My mom always made a big deal about Sunday morning breakfasts. When I was in high school, we'd all sit around the table eating eggs and bacon while my dad tried and failed to do the crossword puzzle, asking us at every turn to help him with clues. These days, though, Sunday brunch was a scattered affair, what with my dad off in the garage performing experiments on my car and my grandma upstairs composing and recomposing her will.

This morning my mom was nobly trying to make waffles.

"Hunter," she said sternly, "you cannot ride the shoe when I'm trying to cook."

My little brother looked up from below, where he was sitting on her foot and latching on to her leg like some overgrown tick. "Giddyup!" he howled.

"Jesus Christ." She sighed, opening a cupboard door and then closing it again. "Oh—pardon my language."

Hunter shrugged. "I don't give a crap."

She dumped water into a bowl of Bisquick. Hunter was still clinging to her leg. "I swear," she said, "it's just completely impossible. Ryden, you were a reasonable kid once. Can't you talk some sense into this one?"

I paused in my ceaseless (and fruitless) perusal of the want ads and held out an orange to Hunter. "Here, little monster," I said coaxingly. "Come get an orange!"

Hunter merely stuck out his tongue at me, remaining stubbornly affixed to my mother.

"He just needs tough love," said my grandma, waltzing into the kitchen with a pair of Jackie O sunglasses perched on top of her blue perm. "Hunter, get off your mother's foot or I'm going to eat your brains."

Hunter looked at her with wide, horrified eyes and quickly obeyed.

"Well, that was effective," my mom said mildly, watching him disappear into the living room. "Thanks, Maureen. That's another year of therapy."

Grandma stuck her finger into the waffle batter and made a face. "For him or for you?"

"For both of us," Mom said, waving Grandma away from the bowl. "As you can see, Hunter's no picnic. He's . . . different."

"No shit, Sherlock," my grandma said, coming to sit beside me at the kitchen table. "I am completely aware of that. Did you know that yesterday at the beauty parlor, he gathered up all the hair clippings, brought them home, and put them in a cardboard box with a blanket and a bowl of milk?"

My mom sighed. "He really wants a rabbit. But I'm not convinced he's ready for the responsibility."

"You're always coddling him, Carmella! Do you want him to grow up to be an even bigger mama's boy than he already is?"

"I don't coddle him," my mom protested. "And can you watch the volume?"

"See? Coddling him."

"Actually, Grandma," I said, putting a hand on her gnarled knuckles, "I don't think it's considered coddling that she doesn't want Hunter to hear you saying bad things about him. I think it's just, you know, *humane*."

Grandma sniffed. "I don't know what that word means," she said. Which I'm quite sure was a lie.

"I'm just concerned about Hunter," my mom said, pouring the batter into the waffle maker. "I think he might be a little . . . strange. Uniquely strange."

Grandma sat up straighter in her chair and knocked her fist on the table. "Damn right he is! He should be. He's a Malby. Strange is good. It indicates a powerful creative force."

My mom did not look comforted. She poured a glass of orange juice and set it on the table in front of me. "Vitamin C," she said. "Drink up."

Then my dad came into the kitchen looking pleased with himself and humming the music from *2001: A Space Odyssey*. Out of tune, I might add.

"Ryden!" he exclaimed, interrupting the musical entertainment. "Come on, I've got something to show you."

I took my time getting out of my chair. Of course, whatever it was that he wanted to show me had to wait until he devoured a waffle straight from the iron, no fork, no syrup, no nothing.

"Follow me," he said, his mouth full.

"Don't try to ride his foot like that brother of yours," Grandma said, a comment I did not dignify with an answer.

My dad washed down his dry waffle with my glass of orange juice and then wiped his mouth on his arm. "The rest of you come, too. Carmella, honey, lay off those delicious waffles for a minute. This is a big deal I'm about to show you!"

We were all used to Dad's little show-off sessions, and though they were never worthy of excitement, we always tried to humor him. (Last weekend he'd called us out to the lawn to see what a big pile of dandelions he'd weeded.) Obediently we followed him in a line as he led us out the front door and onto the driveway. With a grand flourish, he pressed the garage door opener, and we watched as the door screeched its way upward, revealing my little red Escort, practically gleaming, all shiny and put back together again.

"No way, it's really fixed?" I squealed.

My dad nodded proudly. "Your father doesn't dick around. Now I'm going to get in and fire her up and you can just hear that engine purr." He popped the hood and I went to stand dutifully in front of the car, watching as the belts began to turn and the motor began to vibrate and hum. It was a miracle.

I clapped my hands. "I knew you could do it!" Which was not true in the slightest—I had not thought for a second I'd ever drive that car again—but I figured I might as well be positive now that the Escort lived once more.

"Damn straight," my dad yelled. "I'm gonna give her some more gas, gonna rev this baby up!" The engine whined as the RPMs increased. "Whoo-ee!" he cried.

He reached into the car fiddling with something on the dashboard or the gearshift, I couldn't tell, and then suddenly there was a strange grinding noise. The next thing

I knew my car was shooting backward out of the garage, knocking over a trash can on its way out. And then it was still going, down the driveway, and it didn't stop at the sidewalk—oh, no, it kept right on going until it hopped the curb on the other side of the street and smashed into Mr. and Mrs. Ubbin's giant sago palm.

There was a splat.

And then I saw the little pile of cat poop on the driveway, and beside that, a smear of flattened gray fur.

Shitshitshit.

"Oh, dear God," my mom said, putting her hand to her mouth. Grandma covered her face with the corner of her robe and peeked out only warily. I felt sick to my stomach and reached out to my mom to steady myself.

"David's cat," I whispered.

We all stood around it, not sure what to do.

Grandma wiped at her eyes. "It's just not fair. There you are, just this innocent little thing who'd never even hurt a fly"—she pressed her face back into her robe, shielding herself from the carnage—"and the next thing you know, you're murdered by my son, Walter Malby, the man who fixed a car only to wreck it again. Worse than it was wrecked before, I might add."

"It was an accident!" my dad yelled. "Obviously, all of it was. Ryden, why didn't you tell me the cat was there?"

I threw up my hands. "So now it's my fault? I didn't even see the damn thing because you told me I had to watch the engine purr!" I was fuming: it was so like him to want to put the blame on someone else. Had Hunter been around, instead of upstairs vegging out in front of the TV, Dad probably would have told him it was *his* fault— that he'd run over the cat because he was distracted by having such a weird son.

"Oh, so you can't do two things at once? You can't move your eyeballs a little bit to the left or the right?"

I looked from the dead animal to my dead car and back again. "This is ridiculous! You hated that cat! You said you were going to flatten it, and you did!"

My dad stuck his finger out at me and shook it. "Keep your voice down!"

I glanced over at the curtained windows of David's house as my mom ran her fingers through her short red hair, something she did when she was feeling stressed.

"You did say you were going to run that cat over if it took another crap," she pointed out.

"It was a goddamn accident!" my father yelled, not obeying his own "keep your voice down" rule.

"All right, all right," I said. "Let's just calm down, okay? Someone has to go tell the neighbor."

We all looked at my dad, who backed away, shaking his head. "Oh, no," he said. "I don't want to."

"But you have to. You're the responsible party," I said.

He looked at us—daughter, wife, mother—and saw that it was three against one. "What am I going to say? How am I going to tell him?" He gazed down at the cat, which was as flat as a piece of shag carpet. After a few moments he looked back up at us, his face visibly brightening. "I know. I'll tell him in a song. 'Guess who killed your cat today, doo-da, doo-da, guess who killed your cat today, oh doo-da day!'"

"You are not telling him in a song," I hissed, grabbing his elbow. "Come on, I'll go with you. Mom, will you call Triple A and order us a tow truck? And maybe you want to apologize to the Ubbins about the dent they're going to have in their palm tree."

My dad and I trudged across the lawn and stood nervously on David's porch. I rapped gently on the door, because my dad was incapable of doing anything but his "dum da da dum dum—dum dum!" knock, a cheerful summons that seemed no more suited to the occasion than the "Guess who killed your cat today" song.

After a moment the door slowly opened, revealing David's tanned, sleepy face. I drew in my breath—somehow I'd forgotten how handsome he was. "Hello?" he said politely.

"Your cat's dead," my dad blurted.

I cringed and held up my hands. "What he means is—"

But my dad barreled on. "I ran over it with a car. By mistake."

David just stood there, looking stunned.

"We're really so sorry," I added. "We feel awful." When my dad didn't say anything I kicked him in the shin.

"Yes," he parroted. "We feel awful."

Then David stepped onto the porch. He was wearing rumpled khakis and a faded T-shirt. "Where is he?"

"He's in our driveway," my dad said. "Or *on* our driveway would maybe be more accurate. He's sort of stuck there if you know what I mean."

"Jesus, Dad," I said. "Could you be more inappropriate?" I turned to David. "We'll bring him to you," I said. "We'll put him in a box and you can . . . I don't know . . . say good-bye to him or whatever." I was almost in tears. I hadn't really liked the cat, either—it bit me once when I tried to pet it—but I felt horrible that it had been killed.

David looked down at his bare feet. He was obviously upset, but he probably didn't want to show it. "Yes," he said softly. "I guess that's what we should do."

That was how the whole Malby family found itself standing around the hole my dad had dug in David's backyard, while "Memory" from *Cats* piped mournfully out of our portable stereo. (This was courtesy of Hunter, who had a collection of Broadway musical soundtracks. He knew all of *Les Mis* by heart, and was working his way through both *Jesus Christ Superstar* and *Spamalot*.)

I kept watching David, who shifted from foot to foot nervously. His eyes were a little red and swollen.

"Would you like to, uh, say something or something?" my dad asked.

David blinked, looking startled. "Buster was a good cat," he said. "I'm sorry he had to die in such a horrible, violent way."

"I'm sorry he shat on my driveway so much," I heard my dad say under his breath.

"I'll miss him," David said.

"You could always get another one," Hunter said helpfully. He was not too concerned about Buster's demise because he firmly believed that Buster was in a better place, up in kitty heaven chasing angel mice.

My grandma shook her head emphatically. She was wearing an enormous black hat (very funereal) and an orange velour housedress (very 1969). "No, he shouldn't. Cats are only for fat lonely women and gays."

I cringed visibly, but held my tongue. Calling her out for such a prejudice would only encourage her. And at least she didn't say "queers."

My dad stepped forward and handed David a box containing the cat. It said RIP SEÑOR GATO—Hunter had written it, and David hadn't had the heart to explain that Brazilians speak Portuguese—and it was a box from Domino's, because that's how flat the poor thing was.

I felt as though I were playing a role in some absurdist drama as I held my brother's hand and watched David set the box gently into the hole. It went in an inch or two and then stuck.

"It's too big," Hunter said, a fact which was not lost on anyone.

David rotated the box slightly, trying to edge it into the hole, and my father bent down and tried to widen the hole's dimensions a little with a trowel. But that proved too inefficient for him, so after a moment he stood up, brushed off his hands, and then stomped down on the box, stuffing the poor cat into its undignified grave.

My grandma gasped and clutched at her heart. "He's going to do that to *me* someday soon," she whispered, horrified. "He's just going to step on my face and pour dirt over it."

Oh, my God, I thought, *can it get any worse?*

I'll bet you know the answer to that one. Because when my family's involved, things can always get worse.

As my dad began to shovel dirt on top of the box, he noticed a pizza coupon still affixed to it. He reached into the hole. "Twenty-five percent off! Gee, thanks, Buster!" he said brightly, and tucked the coupon into his pocket.

CHAPTER 15

I felt terrible all day, thinking about David and his poor cat. I thought I should go and offer some more words of condolence, so around dinnertime I slipped on a nice sundress and walked over to his house. I guess I had ulterior motives, though, because I carried a bottle of wine under my arm. I intended to offer it as a token of apology, but if he, say, happened to invite me in to drink it, I certainly wouldn't say no. The last person I'd been on a date with—not that this would be a *date,* of course—was Billy Stephens, who worked at the student café on campus and had spent the entire evening talking about what a great snowboarder he was.

When David opened the door I held out the wine and just started talking. "I can't tell you how sorry I am," I said. "About everything. About your poor cat, about that horrendous funeral my dad concocted, and really about my lunatic father in general. I'm sorry you had to move in next to a family of complete weirdos. I don't know how you've put up with all of it. I mean, you never even complained about the busted purple coffin we had sitting in the middle of our front lawn."

David smiled. "Well, the craftsmanship was quite nice," he said. "I mean, what's left of it."

I smiled back, but then I wasn't sure what to say next.

"Do you want some dinner?" he asked, taking the wine from my hands.

The invitation made me bolder. "Depends on what you're having."

"Pancakes," he said. "I like breakfast for dinner."

"Funny," I said. "I like dinner for breakfast. Leftover pizza especially." Then I cringed, thinking of Buster in his pepperoni-stained Domino's box. "Um . . . My name is Ryden, by the way," I said. "Ryden Malby."

"I know. You told me that the other time," he reminded me. "Or the Ryden part, anyway. I figured out the Malby from the name on your mailbox, because I'm clever like that." He stepped aside and ushered me in. "Anyway, come on in, Ryden Malby."

As I stepped into his living room I experienced a strange, almost vertiginous feeling. "It's so weird," I said, shaking my head. "This is exactly like my house, except that everything is flipped. Like, our hall is on that side, and our bay window is on the other . . ."

"Really, exactly like yours?"

"Well, you have better taste than my family," I allowed. "I mean, we have one of those HANG IN THERE kitten posters in our living room."

He laughed. "You're kidding."

"Barely. What we really have are a bunch of pictures of windmills. My dad was really into windmills for a while." I slipped off my sandals and pressed my toes into the soft new carpet. "Also our rugs are totally mismatched. There was this whole Turkish carpet phase, but that transitioned into an interest in sisal and bamboo. Did you know they make rugs out of bamboo fiber?"

"Your father is a . . . unique man," David said diplomatically.

"That's one way of putting it." I followed him into the kitchen and watched as he poured batter onto an electric griddle. "You don't use Bisquick?" I asked.

He shook his head. "Never. It's a sad day when a person can't put together homemade pancake or waffle batter. It involves only about four ingredients."

I stirred the batter in its pretty blue bowl. "Don't tell

that to my mother. She thinks Bisquick *is* homemade. She says we ought to be happy she isn't buying the frozen kind and serving it to us thawed."

"The key to the perfect pancake—besides homemade batter—is flipping it at exactly the right moment. It's a science really. I used to use an egg timer, but now I can do it just by feel." David slid the spatula under the pancakes and flipped them expertly over, revealing perfectly golden surfaces.

"I'm impressed," I said.

"That was the plan," he said.

I wandered around the kitchen and poked my head into the dining room, admiring his funky mid-century modern lamps, his art hanging on the wall, his sturdy teak shelves. It was the home of a real adult, and an adult with good taste. As I fingered the leaves of a thriving rice paper plant, I realized how badly I wanted something like this for myself—a place to make my own

When he'd stacked our plates high with steaming, vanilla-scented pancakes, he led me back into the living room. "I don't like the dining room," he said. "It feels too formal. Plus my friend borrowed all my chairs for a photo shoot, so we'd have to eat standing up."

I pointed to a heap of multicolored plastic near the living room's east wall. "What's that?"

"That? A couch."

I inspected it more closely. "It looks like a giant beach ball died or something." It clashed horribly with David's otherwise excellent décor.

David came over to the pile of plastic, pressed a button, and the thing began to inflate. "Inflate-a-Couch is half the price of a regular sofa, conveniently stores in the closet or under the bed, and can even be used as a flotation device in case of a flood," David said in an oily, smarmy voice. Then he sat down and tapped the spot next to him. "Come on, try it."

Hesitantly I sat down. I didn't want the thing to collapse underneath me, and honestly, it didn't really look that sturdy.

"What do you think?"

"I sort of feel like I'm on an inflatable raft or something."

"Yeah, except that you're not in a pool drinking a daiquiri. It's a piece of crap."

I laughed at his vehemence. "What did you buy it for then?"

"I didn't. I directed the infomercial."

I looked at him more closely. He was so tanned, so fit-looking. I guess I must have thought he was a professional rock climber or tennis instructor or something. "Wow, so that's what you do. It sounds interesting."

"It's not, really," David said, forking the last bite of

pancake into his mouth. He was a very fast eater. "In fact, it's sort of awful. Do you want more breakfast?"

"Thanks, but I'm still working on this stack. How'd you get started doing that?"

He leaned back, and the couch squeaked loudly. "I wanted to be a movie director. Independent, small-budget films. I needed a work visa. I came here with nothing, though, and it was an opportunity."

"I get it," I said, taking a sip of wine. Surprisingly, it didn't go so terribly with pancakes. "You get a paycheck and access to all the equipment you'd need to have for your own film. That makes sense."

David nodded absently. "Then flash, it's three years later, and I'm doing ads for the Hula Chair, the ButtMeister, and a robotic toothbrush they call the Dent-A-Fun 2000. And I don't stop, because by now I'm used to the paycheck. It's not as if I could pay the mortgage by working in a video store like Quentin Tarantino or whoever while I made my brilliant art-house flick." He took my plate from me and walked toward the kitchen. "What's the expression— golden handcuffs?" he asked over his shoulder.

"Don't ask me," I said. "I'm not real experienced on the job-slash-paycheck front." I heard him clattering around in the kitchen and I drank a little more wine. I would have thought I'd feel nervous, but I didn't. On one of the shelves nearby I noticed a picture of David holding a pretty little girl with lovely dark ringlets on his lap. "Who's the girl?" I asked.

David reappeared, drying his hands on a towel. "That's my daughter. Carolina. She just turned four. That picture is from the time we went to Peru."

I scanned the room, looking for evidence of a child and seeing none. "Oh. Does she—she doesn't—"

David smiled wistfully. "She lives with her mother in Brazil. We're divorced."

"Oh, I'm sorry," I said, even though I wasn't sorry—at least not about the divorced part. "Well, you must go back to see her a lot." I tried to sound cheerful.

He looked pensively at his hands. His fingernails were short and very clean. "Not for . . . eleven months. Oh, God," he said, touching his brow. "That's almost a year." He was silent for a moment, and then seemed to shake off the thoughts that were making him sad. "Enough about me. Your turn. What is Ryden Malby doing with her life?"

I sighed. "I don't know why everyone's asking me that lately. But you know what? It's just great, David. Really exhilarating. I've been turned down at every magazine or publishing company in the L.A. area, as well as at two insurance agencies. My car got smashed, then my dad fixed it, and then he ran it into a tree. I lost my job peddling luggage. And I live with my parents. Also my grandma, who can be as mean as a snake, and my little brother, who may or may not be completely insane."

David laughed. "Living the dream, I see," he said. He looked at me with eyes that were dark and—well, not to be too cliché about it, but—smoldering. I mean, really, they *smoldered,* like little black fires.

I leaned back and took a long drink of my wine. I saw him notice my legs under my sundress, and I stretched them somewhat ostentatiously. I wasn't sure where this was going, but I was enjoying myself for the first time in weeks. "The whole postgraduation thing isn't turning out exactly as I'd planned it, that's for sure," I allowed.

David kept his gaze on my calves. "But nothing is ever how we plan it, is it?" he said softly.

I leaned back on the plastic couch and closed my eyes. "I was just so sure I'd be doing something incredible by now," I said. "Or at least doing *something.* I mean, what's going on here? Do I have to do phone sex lines or something? I hear they're always hiring."

David cleared his throat. "Well, listen," he said. "I know it doesn't solve the problem, but if you need something temporary, we can always use an extra PA on set. Production assistant—do you know what that is? The hours are crap, and the money's pretty bad, but it'll get you out of the house. I could get you on the next project. It starts the first week in August."

His offer touched me. "Really?" I asked, turning to him. That was only a week away, which meant only seven more days of doing nothing. "You'd do that for me?"

"Sure," he said. "I like to help a friend out. So now that that's settled, let's focus on the good things."

"Okay, like what?" I said, feeling even better now. "I'm game."

He leaned toward me. "Well, for instance, your ears."

I shot him a suspicious look. "What do you mean, my ears?"

"Well, they're just fantastic," he said, reaching out and touching one gently with his fingertip.

"Are you some kind of weird fetishist?" I asked teasingly. (Though maybe in the back of my mind I was a *trifle* worried. After all, I now knew there were men who liked beans on women's feet and stuffed baby giraffes.)

David laughed. "Not in the slightest. You just have these perfect little ears. These flawless, amazing little ears."

No one in my life had ever noticed my ears. Who knew if I really had nice ones or ugly ones—and who cared? All that mattered was that this gorgeous Brazilian was admiring them, and I was feeling the warmth of the wine in my stomach and the first sense of optimism I'd had in weeks. I drew in my breath, leaned forward, and kissed him on the mouth.

It seemed to take him by surprise, but he caught up pretty quickly, and soon his hands were in my hair and mine were on his waist, and I was tasting the sweetness of maple syrup and wine on his lips.

He buried his face in my neck and then I could feel his hands moving up my legs, teasing and tickling along the hem of my skirt, and then I felt them slide higher and higher. Gently I pushed him up and off me, and then, when he was sitting up, leaning against the squeaking plastic couch, I threw one leg across his lap and straddled him.

I bent down to kiss him and I smelled the clean piney scent of his skin. His hands moved up my back and then tangled themselves up in my hair.

It had been so long since I'd kissed anyone. Even this was enough to leave me breathless.

"Your lips are perfect, too," David whispered. "And your mouth and your tongue . . ."

"Mmmm," I said, bending down to kiss beneath his chin.

I could feel his hands reaching to unhook my bra. He did so expertly, and I was getting ready to lift my dress over my head, throwing all caution to the wind, when I heard something behind me. I didn't make much of it—it was only enough to make me pause for a moment. And then I was pulling my dress up and David was making little sounds of pleasure into my chest—

"What the hell is going on?"

My father stood in the middle of the living room, looking for all the world like a bull rhino about to charge. Behind him, my mother carried a platter of cookies, and my grandma and Hunter brought up the rear, each holding a clutch of daisies from our garden.

"Oh, fuck me," David said.

"I would, but it looks like someone beat me to it!" Grandma said, looking surprisingly unruffled.

I pulled my dress down and scrambled off David's lap. "What are you doing here?" I cried. My face was scarlet, I could feel it.

"We came to pay our condolences," my mother said stiffly. My dad was red in the face, too, and possibly too angry to say anything.

"You could have knocked," I said. "That's normally what people do."

"I could sense you were up to no good!" my dad bellowed. "I would have busted the door down, so good thing it was open!"

I turned back to David, mouthing, *I'm sorry, I'm sorry.* He had a small and I hoped sympathetic smile on his face. "I should go," I said helplessly.

"Of course," he said.

"Thanks for the pancakes," I whispered, and then shoved my family toward the front door. My mom set the cookies on the table in the hall and my dad picked them back up.

"Not leaving cookies for sex perverts," he muttered.

I wanted to protest—hello, David was not a pervert! I was the one to come on to him!—but I thought it was better not to fight. Better just to get him the hell out of there.

When we were outside, heading back to our house, Hunter reached up and tugged on my mom's dress. "What were they doing in there? Was Ryden wrestling that man? I like to wrestle. Why didn't they let me play? I'm a good wrestler."

My mother shot me a look: *Now I've got to lie to him!* "Yes, Hunter," she said. "Your sister and that man were playing a funny game, but now they're finished and Ryden is coming home with us."

"Who won the funny game?" Hunter asked.

"No one," I told him. "It was a tie."

My dad reached for my arm and held me back while the rest of them went inside. He looked into my eyes. "Tell me you used a rubber," he said.

"A what?" I was shocked.

"A rubber. You know, a raincoat? A Johnny bag? A love glove?" His voice rose in pitch and volume.

"Oh, my God," I said, burying my head in my hands. I couldn't believe I was hearing this. My ears—the very ears that David thought were so amazing—would never be the same.

"A condom, Ryden," my father yelled. "Did you use a condom?"

"What are you talking about? I didn't even—"

He didn't wait for me to finish. "Because herpes is no picnic. And it's not a river-rafting trip, either, like those commercials make you think."

I couldn't help it, I started to laugh. *"What?"*

He pointed his finger right in my face. "No more! That's it. Ix-nay on his oodle-day."

"Oodle-day?"

"Doodle! His pecker! His one-eyed trouser snake! His baloney pony! His pork sword!"

I covered my ears. "No more," I begged, "no more."

"Weiner!" my dad said, just for emphasis. "You're not seeing him again." He shook his finger at me. "Do you hear me?"

I turned on him, eyes flashing. "Or you're going to do what? Ground me? I don't see how my life could get much worse than it is right now, so why don't you go ahead and try? Why don't you ground your twenty-two-year-old daughter and see how well that works?"

"You live in my goddamn house, young lady!" he cried.

I opened the front door and was greeted by the room uncannily like the one I'd been inches away from getting naked in. There were Dad's dumb windmill pictures; our old green sofa we sat on to watch television; the striped love seat Hunter barfed on after his fifth birthday party; and the fireplace you couldn't use ever since a raccoon got stuck and died in it. All the things I thought I'd have left behind by now.

"Did you hear me, Ryden? You live in my house!" my dad repeated.

"Believe you me, I'm going to do everything I can to change that," I said. Then I stomped up the stairs, leaving my father fuming in the foyer while my mom fluttered around him, trying to placate him with the cookies meant for David.

CHAPTER 16

"He said *what*?" Adam howled into the phone.

I flopped back on my bed, landing in a warm patch of summer sunlight. "One-eyed trouser snake," I said miserably.

"You have *got* to get out of there," he said.

"Tell me about it," I said. I knew I could count on Adam to commiserate with me about the horrors of my family, but something stopped me from telling him the truth about the David situation. Instead I led him to believe that my dad had been counseling me to avoid the male genitalia in general, rather than one particular set of it.

"Let's go get lunch," he said.

"Let's go shopping," I countered. I expected him to ask me what I thought I was doing shopping when I didn't have two nickels to rub together, but he simply said, "Okay. See you in a flash."

He showed up half an hour later, freshly showered, wearing a faded button-down with his sandy hair falling over his green eyes. As we walked to his car, an ancient Toyota that looked as if it would barely make it out of the driveway, I glanced over at David's house. The shades were drawn and a newspaper lay on the porch. *Is he still asleep?* I wondered. Or was he lying in bed awake, thinking about the neighbor girl he very nearly slept with?

I shook off the thought—the embarrassment of my dad walking in on us was too much. I knew I'd have to get over it, though, because I'd be working for him in a matter of days.

"So where are we going?" Adam asked, opening my door for me.

"Melrose," I said, ducking inside.

Adam raised his eyebrows at me but made no comment.

Inside Lily, a very chic boutique with lime-green walls and a silk-paneled dressing room, I tried on dress after dress: a swishy lemon one, a ruffled periwinkle one, a classic little black one . . . I loved them all, and so I stood, half-naked, and gazed at the pile of them longingly.

"So what's this thing again exactly?" Adam said. "You're going to be a PA now?" I could see his feet pacing back and forth over the sheepskin rug.

"It's only temporary," I said. "Our neighbor hooked me up."

"Your neighbor? That dude whose cat you killed?"

"The dude whose cat my *dad* killed. Yes. He's really nice."

"I'm surprised he'd want to do you a favor after what your car did to his cat."

"Maybe he thinks I'm charming," I said.

There was silence from the other side of the door. I slipped a mocha-colored silk sheath with a plunging neckline over my head and then stepped out of the dressing room.

"Zip me?" I said.

I felt Adam's fingers at the small of my back as he reached for the zipper and slid it gently up. Even though his hands were warm, I felt a little shiver travel across my skin.

Then I turned around and smiled.

"Wow," Adam said, looking me up and down. "That's really something."

"You like?" I asked. I looked down to see—miracle of

miracles—some very nice cleavage. Clearly this was the dress I was meant to have.

"Definitely." He grinned. "Hey, so Thursday night's gig, remember? I wrote a little something-something for you."

"For me? Shut up. Do you think I should get a matching handbag?"

"I'm serious," Adam said. "Do you want a little preview?"

He didn't wait for me to answer, but opened his mouth and began to sing. Loudly. "Ryden's beautiful, it's true / Her eyes are so big and blue / And then one day I touched her boob / And things got really awwwwkward."

I threw one of my socks at him. What he said was true, but we'd been freshmen in college when it happened. We'd both been very drunk, and after a day or two of blushing every time we caught each other's eye, we got over it quickly enough. "You're an idiot," I said, laughing. I couldn't help but notice how the salesgirls— who were applauding his efforts—seemed to be sending admiring glances in his direction.

"You love me," he said.

"Always," I said breezily, ducking back into the dressing room.

"So listen," he called. "Here's the plan. You, me, and that dress. First, I totally kick ass at the show." He tossed my sock over the top of the dressing room door. "Second, you throw your bra onstage and scream like a maniac. Try to make sure it's a nice bra, though, and not some ugly Playtex thing you inherited from your grandma. Third—this is the goods right here—we celebrate your new quasi-temporary-whatever job with a nice dinner. I'm talking a restaurant with cloth napkins, multiple forks, and everything."

"It sounds pretty nice," I said. "That'll be my first day of work, you know. As a PA. What if I'm, like, exhausted?"

"Well, you'll have to drink some coffee, because it's going to be the best night of your life."

"You must be buying then," I said.

"But of course," he said, sounding very gallant. Then he whispered, "When we go to the restaurant? Just don't order the *pork sword*. I hear they overcook it."

I blazed out of the dressing room, back in my summer uniform of a skirt and a tank top. "Ewww, ewww, ewww," I said, punching him. "You're disgusting."

"You love me," he said again.

"Bah!" I said.

I arrived home to find my dad standing in the driveway whirling a pair of nunchucks over his head.

"Stop, please," I cried, "before you kill yourself."

Surprisingly, he did stop—though not without knocking himself in the gut first. "Ow," he said.

"What in the world are you doing?" I asked.

"What does it look like? I'm practicing methods of attack and defense."

"In our driveway? What for?" I set down the bag with my lovely new dress and took the nunchucks from his hand.

"Nothing. A minor bit of aggression from a buckle competitor."

I gave him a questioning look.

My dad took a sip of his SuperMax energy drink. (My mom had gotten a case of the stuff on deep discount, but it was so disgusting Dad was the only one willing to drink it.) "Some whack job by the name of Buckle-O-Bill says that the buckles I bought and paid for are stolen property," he said. "He had the nerve to come to my house and tell me that a box of his belt buckles went missing a couple of weeks ago, and that he has it on good information that they ended up in my hands. He stands there in his stupid cowboy outfit and tries to tell me that they're all his. He says he's the only person in the whole United Freaking States of America who makes buckles with the state of Delaware on them. Ditto buckles with two porcupines mating, which is another buckle that I am lucky enough to have in my box of buckles from Gary. *Which I bought and paid for.*"

"So what did you do?" I couldn't help but hope that he'd done the sensible thing, which was to accept that the belt buckles probably *were* the property of this Buckle-O-Bill—after all, Gary did not strike one as, like, the honest type—and come to some sort of agreement with the man.

My dad grabbed the nunchucks back and stuck them in his pocket. "I told him to get the hell off my property before I rendered him unconscious with one jab from my fingers to his neck."

I sighed. "Oh, Dad, why did you do that? That was a horrible idea! And anyway, have you ever really tried that trick?"

"I tried it on Adam in the restaurant, remember? He fainted." My dad made the gesture: two fingers aimed right at my jugular.

I rolled my eyes. "Dad, he *faked* it."

My dad looked unfazed. "Not how I remember it," he said.

What could a person say to a man so clearly out of touch with reality? I held up my bag from Lily. "I bought a new dress," I said.

My dad peered inside. "Kinda the color of cat shit, isn't it?"

Someone please just kill me now, I thought.

CHAPTER 17

"It's as easy as *uno, dos, tres!*" proclaimed the mustachioed, sombrero-sporting *campesino* on the soundstage. He held up an avocado, smiled, and then plunged it into the funnel of a great big red machine sporting the words "The Guacanator 3000." "No peeling, no pitting—the Guacanator does it all for you," the man exclaimed in a thick Spanish accent. "Making guacamole for your family, for a party, or just for your own self has never been easier!" He pressed a button shaped like a chili pepper, and a stream of green goo vomited out from the Guacanator's spout. He stuck his finger into the goo and then into his mouth. "Mmm, delicious! Just like my mama down in Mexico used to make.

Mira, it's always a fiesta with Señor Guacanator. I, Juan Garcia, promise you that!"

I set the crate of avocados I'd just hauled in from the supermarket down on the floor, close to the counter where the Guacanator was situated but out of camera range. "Avocados on set," I said into my walkie-talkie, feeling a giddy wave of excitement. I'd been a PA for four hours by now. It was a great job, as long as you didn't mind getting yelled at, ordered around, and generally being treated like a serf. Which I didn't, because I was finally earning a paycheck. Granted, a small one—but a paycheck nonetheless. In another three days I'd be able to pay off the lovely new mocha dress I was wearing. (Which, by the way, was not the best wardrobe choice for schlepping avocados around.)

I glanced over at David, who was standing near the cameraman and observing the performance with a look of mild boredom. As I watched, a guy in a suit—some ad executive or something, I assumed—came over and whispered something in David's ear. David bit his lip, nodded, and then held up his hand. "Cut," he yelled.

The *campesino* ripped off his sombrero and then his fake mustache. "Oh, balls," he said, his voice suddenly without a trace of Spanish inflection. "This mustache is ruining my performance. The little hairs keep falling off and getting into my mouth!" David tried to look patient. "All right, we'll see what we can do. Maybe makeup has a backup mustache or something. We'll deal with that. But right now, everyone take five."

The ad executive glanced down at his watch and frowned. Ignoring him, David walked toward the water cooler, shaking his head.

I'd been shy around David all day—we'd never mentioned the embarrassment of last Sunday—but he looked like he could use some cheering up, so I walked over and smiled. The fake *campesino* bore down on us.

"Ground control to director David," I said, holding on to the mic of my headset. "We have an asshole incoming. Repeat, incoming asshole. Roger that."

David rubbed his tired-looking eyes and gave me a halfhearted chuckle.

"I think the director needs his space, Juan," I said as he approached, putting up a hand.

"It's not Juan," he replied. "It's Peter and I'm from goddamn New Rochelle, New York." After glaring at us for another few seconds, he turned around and went to complain to someone else.

"So how's the first day on the job?" David asked. "As shitty as I promised?"

I grabbed a handful of M&M's from a big plastic bowl of them. "I'm having fun. And I like any place with free candy. How's it going with you?"

"Great," David said. Then he rubbed his eyes again. "Actually not great."

I held out my palm of M&M's and he took a red one. "Yeah, I could kind of tell."

David's cell rang and he answered curtly. "Yes, uh-huh. Right."

He looked highly peeved, so when he hung up I asked him what it was about.

"The account manager—that's the guy in the suit over there—says not to start rolling again until I talk to him about strategy."

I looked over at the guy who'd spoken to David when he was standing by the camera. "That's the guy who just called you? But he's, like, fifty feet away. He couldn't just walk over and tell you what he needed to tell you?"

"Welcome to the pissing contest of middling ad executives on infomercials. Pathetic, isn't it?" David said, and stalked over to the suit.

I went to find Peter/Juan, who was over by the craft service table. I held out my palm. "All right, where's that mustache? Let me see if I can figure out the problem."

"Hell if I know," Peter/Juan said. "I stuck it on a pole somewhere." He picked up a sandwich from a stack of them on a plastic tray and held it to his nose and sniffed. "You've got to call this caterer, man," he said. "These sandwiches smell like someone was carrying them in their freaking Jockey shorts. You know, like maybe right between their ass cheeks?" He waved the sandwich at me, offering me proof, and I backed away slightly, trying to maintain some modicum of professionalism.

"I'll go talk to someone," I said. "Hang on right there."

"Tell them no more ass-crack sandwiches, okay? How about some salami or a goddamn turkey club?" Peter/ Juan called.

I walked over to where David was standing with the ad man.

"First of all," the ad guy was saying, "I'm going to need more Mexican. *Andale, andale, arriba arriba!* That kind of thing. You've got to get people excited about guacamole."

David's voice was coolly ironic. "Guacamole is by nature quite exciting, Robert."

Robert stared at him. "Tell me, are the smart-ass comments included in your fee, or do I pay extra for that?"

David looked up at the ceiling, clearly wanting to respond but holding himself back.

"And while we're at it, your shots are boring. We're not selling panty hose on QVC here. The Guacanator is a *high-tech one-of-a-kind secret weapon of the kitchen*. So I want you to spice up the camera work, okay? Like that shot in *The Matrix* where Keanu jumps up and the camera does a three-sixty around him. That's exciting. I say we do that, but instead of Keanu, it's the Guacanator. The wave of the future for guacamole."

David clapped his hands together. "You know, that's a brilliant idea. And maybe while I'm at it, I could film the Guacanator flying around in a big red cape! Or wait, how about we catch it tossing the One Ring into the fires of Mount Doom? Or hoist it up on a cross and we could have *The Passion of the Avocado?*"

Robert stared at David. "Do you think that's funny?"

David snorted. "Do you know what I think? I think you're an idiot. I quit." He yanked off his headset, turned around, and grabbed my arm. "Come on, Ryden," he said. "We're getting the hell out of here."

CHAPTER 18

Two margaritas later, it was as if the Guacanator, Peter/
Juan, and Robert the idiot ad executive had never existed.
David leaned back in his wrought-iron chair, happily sur-
veying the flowery, palm-strewn courtyard of his favorite
little Mexican café in Malibu.

"I should come here every day," he mused. "Work on
that screenplay I've been thinking about. Start blocking
out the shots."

"That sounds great," I said, dipping a chip in a bowl of
spicy salsa. "Join the ranks of the wannabes."

"Hey, I've got an in," David countered. "Robert the ad
man is also a producer of independent movies!"

I laughed. "Really bad ones, no doubt. Like, a Lindsay Lohan biopic or something."

"No doubt," David agreed. "I hate that guy."

"Remember how he said he needed more Mexican?" I said. "As if Mexican were a language? I mean, like, yeah, *Don Quixote* was written in Mexican."

"You know, he thought I was Mexican," David said. He'd ordered guacamole, but not to eat. "I just want to stare at it spitefully," he'd said.

I fished around in my purse for a Tums—I love salsa, but it doesn't love me—and said, "I swear, I don't know how people like him become executives while people like me are apparently unemployable."

David patted my hand paternally. "You'll figure it out. You're a smart girl."

"But what should I do now?" I asked. "The one decent job I got I worked less than a day at, thanks to you."

I thought back on all my failed interviews. I didn't understand how one person—one *smart* person, if I may say so—could be so roundly rejected. What could I do next? I supposed I could sign up for temp work. I could call the families I used to babysit for and see if they still needed any help. Or I could beg for my old job back at Luggage World. Of course, none of it sounded good in the slightest. The problem was, I still held on to the idea that I could do something meaningful.

"I know what you should do," David said. "I've got the answer to all your problems. You just have to come with me." He held out his hand and helped me up.

And that's how I found myself speeding down the Pacific Coast Highway with the wind blowing through my hair, just like in the movies, a handsome Brazilian by my side and two bottles of Champagne (French, not that fake California stuff) in the backseat.

David was practically giddy, and whether it was the margaritas or his new freedom it was hard to say. "I walked off set today," he kept saying. "I just walked off!"

"If it makes you this happy you should quit stuff more often," I said, pulling down the visor and checking my lip gloss in the mirror.

"That's a very interesting idea, PA Ryden."

"*Ex*-PA Ryden," I reminded him. "And I'm kind of mad at you, you know."

David looked over at me and smiled. "I'll make it up to you."

I crossed my arms and pretended to frown. I liked the idea of David feeling like he owed me something.

As we drove north, seagulls floated above us in the blue sky, calling to one another, and I could smell the briny surf. To my right the green hills glowed emerald in the slowly setting sun.

"Beach?" he asked. "I don't go there enough."

"Me, either," I said. "It's sad—I live in L.A., yet I never see famous people and I never go to the ocean. What else is this place known for?"

"Smog," David answered.

But there was no smog anywhere that evening. The air was warm and crystal clear, and we hit the sand just as the whole sky was turning pink and gold.

"This is what they call the magic hour," David said, kicking off his shoes. "The hour when anything you film is bathed in this gorgeous, melancholy light."

I took off my shoes, too, relishing the soft sand on my feet. It was still warm. "It doesn't look melancholy to me," I said. "It looks perfect."

"Yes," David said, gazing at me. "It does." Then he popped the cork off one of the Champagne bottles and handed it to me. "Take a swig!"

I obeyed, feeling the cool fizz fill my mouth. "I love Champagne," I sighed.

"The whole bottle's yours. See? I've got my own." He popped the cork on that one, too, sending it flying into the air. "We'll drink out of the bottles, because it's fun that way and because we don't have any cups."

But instead of taking a sip, he took off his shirt and tossed it onto the sand. His skin looked like it was made of copper, and the gathering dusk made blue shadows along his muscular arms. I drew in my breath. He smiled at me, and then took off his jeans so he was down to his boxers, and in the next moment he was racing toward the surf, waving his arms in the air and yelling. At the water's edge he hesitated for just one moment, and then he plunged in.

I ran toward the water after him, carrying my Champagne, and as he rose from the waves he held his arms out. "Come on in, it's gorgeous."

"No way," I called. "My dress is new."

He shrugged. "So then take it off."

He looked so childish, so happy—not to mention so handsome—that I did, feeling grateful that my mother had basically forced me to wear a full-length slip underneath the dress because she thought it was more professional that way. I folded up my dress and laid it on the sand as the wind blew my silk slip tight against my body.

At the water's edge I touched a toe to the surf and then pulled back. "Forget it," I said. "Not to be a spoilsport, but that ocean is just too cold."

David reached down and splashed me and I shrieked, backing away. Then he rushed toward me and scooped me up in his arms, and before I could say anything to stop him he had carried me into the waves and let go.

The water was freezing and I came up spluttering and cursing and laughing. "I'm going to kill you," I said.

"You'll have to catch me first," he said.

I grabbed my dress and chased him up the beach, back

to where I'd left my shoes and David had left most of his clothes. David collapsed onto the sand. "Okay," he panted, "you got me. You can kill me now."

"I will just as soon as I have some of this Champagne," I said, sinking down beside him. We drank from our respective Champagne bottles. The wind rose up and blew my hair across my face, and he brushed it away with the tip of his finger.

"You know what I thought when I met you?" He raised his eyebrows playfully as he slipped his clothes back on. "Well, of course at first I thought the obvious things. She's stunning, totally stunning. And smart. And funny. And she gets it—you know? She just gets it."

I bit my lip, feeling shy and thrilled. "And then you thought, wow, she's got an insane family," I said, trying to diffuse the moment a little. I like compliments as much as any girl, but I was a little embarrassed.

David waved that away. "And then I noticed something else. Something subtle, but unmistakable."

I took a big gulp from my Champagne bottle. "Maybe we should just stop at stunning?"

He grinned at me. "I see a girl who has the whole world at her fingertips and she doesn't even know it."

Now that was too much. How could I have the world at my fingertips when the world didn't even want me to earn a paycheck? When the world gave me a dad who came up with one harebrained scheme after another, a mom too busy to stop him, a grandma obsessed with death and hats, and a little brother who licks people's heads? "I don't," I whispered. "Stop."

"Okay," he said. And then he leaned forward and took my face in his hands and kissed me. His lips were soft and warm, and I felt like I was melting into them.

And this time, my crazy family wasn't there to stop me.

CHAPTER 19

David and I kissed on the sand until darkness fell all around us and we'd both finished our Champagne. Then the breeze kicked up and I began to shiver, and David said it seemed like we ought to go. I agreed, and I made him promise to turn the heat on in the convertible, even though it was August.

We drove home in the cool night air, heater blasting. David reached over the gearshift and touched my hand lightly. "So today didn't turn out so bad, did it?"

I leaned back in the leather seat and ran my fingers through my salty, tangled hair. "Nope," I said. "I'm so glad we didn't stay on set and eat those rotten sandwiches."

"I hope they all got food poisoning." David laughed. "I hope they barfed up rotten meat and guacamole all afternoon."

"Especially Robert," I said. "And I hope Peter/Juan choked on his fake mustache."

As we wound down into the Valley and through the streets to our neighborhood, I felt sleepy and calm.

"You don't want to come in, do you?" David asked as he pulled into his driveway.

I shook my head. It didn't feel right, somehow, and I think David knew that, too. He was gorgeous and kind and intelligent, but somehow to do more than enjoy a tipsy make-out session would have seemed like . . . too much. Was it our twelve-year age difference? The fact that our bathroom windows practically looked into each other's? I told myself that I'd figure it out later. "No, I should go to bed. I've got to get up early and look for more jobs." I said this without a trace of irony. I still had the dress to pay off.

"Is it rude of me not to drive you home?"

"Very funny. I think I can make it across the lawn," I said.

He looked at me seriously for a moment. "You know that you'll find what you're looking for, don't you?"

I bit my lip; I felt shy all of a sudden. "What do you mean?"

He just smiled at me, and kissed me on the cheek. "Good night," he said.

"Night," I whispered.

I walked across the lawn barefoot, swinging my sandals in my hand, feeling tired and weirdly optimistic. Maybe David was right. Maybe I would find what I was looking for—a new job, a new place, a new sense of possibility.

"Hey," said a voice.

I looked up to see Adam sitting in the shadows of our porch. "Hey, you, what are you doing here?" I said.

He didn't reply right away, and that's when I remembered. I gasped. "Oh, my God, I'm such an idiot! Oh, no, I totally forgot?" I rushed forward and collapsed onto the porch step beside him, reaching for his hand.

He pulled it away. "Whatever," he said. "It's cool." His voice was distant. Cold, even. "I just came over because I wanted to make sure you were okay. You usually don't fail to show up someplace, or fail to even answer your phone."

I felt almost sick with guilt. "I turned it off. I'm so sorry. I can't believe I forgot your show."

"Whatever, it's fine." He stared out over the lawn.

"How did it go? Were you amazing?"

"It was fine," he repeated, though clearly it wasn't. He got up and started walking to his car.

"Oh, my God," I moaned, "and our dinner. I missed our multifork dinner."

Adam turned back. "Really, you're getting overly worked up about this, Ryden. It's cool, you were busy hanging out with your, um, next-door neighbor, I guess?"

I stood up and held out my hands. "No, it wasn't like that. We were at work, and there was this blowup, and we just took off. It was totally impulsive."

"Uh-huh. Awesome. Well, see you later." He reached for his keys and opened the door.

I went after him, and the cold driveway on my bare feet made me shiver. "Wait. What are you doing?"

"What does it look like?"

"Hold on—please. Let me explain."

Adam slammed the car door shut in anger. "Explain? What exactly needs an explanation, Ryden? The fact that I've been waiting around like a complete idiot, hoping that one day you'll actually feel about me the way I do about you? Or the fact that you're so busy obsessing over your future that you completely forget about the people you're supposed to give a shit about?"

"Adam," I said desperately, "please—"

He cut me off. "Well, guess what. I'm not waiting around anymore. I'm done, okay? I made my decision. I may not know exactly what my future looks like, but I do know one thing: you're not going to be in it." He opened the car door again, got in, and started the engine. The headlights blinded me. "See you around, Ryden," he said, and then peeled out of the driveway and disappeared down the street.

I sank to my knees, reeling in disbelief. I couldn't believe I'd forgotten Adam's show, forgotten our dinner, forgotten everything. I'd never seen him so angry before, and it was all my fault. I put my head in my hands. My lovely night had taken a serious turn for the worse.

Which is why I hardly blinked when the cops showed up, blue and red lights flashing across the quiet neighborhood. Arrest me, I almost yelled. Arrest me for being a horrible friend.

But they hadn't come for me. They'd come for my dad.

CHAPTER 20

"You have the right to remain silent," said the tall cop with the big mustache. "Anything you say can and will be used against you in a court of law."

But my father, who had a slice of pizza in his hand (the remains of his typical late-night snack), was not at all interested in exercising his right to remain silent. "I told you, I had no idea those were hot! I bought and paid for them! I got them from Gary!" He waved the pizza at the policeman for emphasis, and a single piece of pepperoni went sailing off into the night.

The policemen were unimpressed, and obviously had no

idea who Gary was. Meanwhile, Buckle-O-Bill was rifling through the box of buckles, chuckling to himself. "Oh, man, am I glad to have these babies back. Look here, fellas! I made this one to commemorate the appearance of Priscilla Presley on *Dancing with the Stars*. It was the rumba that was the death of her. She shoulda stuck with the tango or the foxtrot. Those were more her style. The rumba is too slutty. You know, I was a real fan of her ex-husband. I saw him in Vegas fourteen times, and I don't care what they say about him getting fat and constipated and dying alone on a toilet seat, that man was a *god*."

No one was paying any attention to him, but that didn't stop him from chattering on and on. When he finally realized how little anyone cared about his ramblings, he tried to give the cops a couple of buckles with stags' heads on them, "for souvenirs of the raid," he said. The officers politely declined.

"I'm telling you, it was an honest transaction," my dad yelled as the tall cop helped him into the backseat of the squad car.

My mother had gathered up her purse and her keys and was standing beside the Le Baron. "Come on, get in," my mother said, ushering Hunter, still in his pajamas, into the backseat.

My grandma appeared in the doorway, wearing a robe

so fuzzy and brown she looked like an ancient, shrunken Bigfoot. "What are they doing with my son?" she yelled.

"Get in the car, Maureen," my mom said. "They're taking him to the station and we're going, too. If they want one Malby, they're going to get them all. Ryden, put your shoes on. You know how dirty police stations are."

"Actually, Mom, I don't. Believe it or not, I've never been arrested," I said, clambering into the front seat and slipping on my sandals. I rubbed my temples. The buzz from the Champagne had faded, and in its place had come fatigue and a deep sense of dread about how the night ahead of us would unfold.

My grandma leaned out the backseat window, pointing at the cops. "Just so you know, I had no part in this! Ask anyone. They'll all tell you: I hate crime."

"Well, we won't mention to them how you 'forgot' to pay for those slippers the other day at Wal-Mart, now, will we?" my mom hissed.

"Oh, for crissake, Carmella, it was a mistake," my grandma said, pulling her head back in. "And they were only four dollars anyway. It's not like I put a real dent in Sam Walton's pocketbook."

"Grandma, who is Sam Walton?" Hunter asked from the backseat. He was holding a teddy bear and looking very sleepy and confused.

"He is a very smart man who figured out how to make children work for two pennies and a crust of bread a day so that you could have sneakers that light up on the bottom," Grandma said, smiling beatifically.

"Maureen, don't talk garbage," my mom said. "We love Wal-Mart."

"But I don't have sneakers that light up on the bottom," Hunter howled. "And I want some really really badly!"

I could not take one more minute of them. "Can you all just shut up?" I cried.

And for once, they actually did.

A very surly woman in civilian clothes led us into the police station's lounge area, which was a horrible little room painted olive green, filled with uncomfortable plastic chairs and lit by fluorescent lights clearly designed to make everyone look their ugliest and most criminal.

Another officer with a mustache came in carrying coffee in a Styrofoam cup for my mother.

"So here's what we're looking at," he said. "We've got to hold your husband, because trafficking in stolen property is no small crime. Bail will be set tomorrow, so you'll be able to take him home then." He looked sternly around at us, stroking his mustache, and I wondered if upper-lip facial hair was part of the Burbank policeman's uniform.

"If we can afford it," my grandma mumbled.

My mother stood up, eyes blazing. "You're going to keep him overnight? You're kidding me. My husband is not a crook—he's just a moron! He had no idea those buckles were stolen!"

"I'm sorry, ma'am, but protocol is protocol." He nodded his head curtly and then walked out.

My grandma took the coffee out of my mom's hands and said, "I told you back in 1976. I said *Do. Not. Marry. Walter. Malby.*"

My mom looked incredulous. "But he's your son!"

Grandma shrugged. "I did the best with what I was given. It's the genes, Carmella. His father was a bona fide imbecile. But oh, he was so handsome!"

I took my phone from my purse and punched in a familiar set of numbers. "Adam," I said, when his voice mail picked up. "I know it's late, and I'm sorry that this is the fifth time I've called you tonight, but I just need to talk. Call me back, will you?"

Then I stared at the phone for a really long time, as if I could make it ring, but it remained silent. I called again and left another message. "Which would you rather be, a bear or a lion? What if you had to be in a circus? Would you bite the hands that feed you?"

I so desperately wanted to talk to him. I wanted to apologize again for missing the Mint show, and I wanted to tell him that if he thought having a father who slept with his cashiers was bad, he should try having one who trafficked in stolen belt buckles and earned himself a bed in the county jail.

My brother clambered up on the chair beside me. "I'm hungry," he whined. "Where's Dad? Why can't we go home?" He squeezed his teddy tightly.

I looked into his big brown eyes and felt very sorry for him. What had he done to deserve a family like this? I reached out and gently ruffled his hair. But then he started to chew on the edge of the chair, and I was reminded that he was maybe the craziest of all of us. "Dad's . . . um, Dad's just getting a tour of the facility. He's going to make sure the beds are really comfortable." Hunter looked dubious, but he didn't say anything to protest.

Grandma said, "Speaking of beds . . . how about we go get in ours?" She pulled the belt of her robe tight around her waist. "Me and my bunions are getting sleepy."

But my mom, who typically gave in to my grandma for the sake of domestic harmony, shook her head. "You might as well get cozy in that robe of yours, Maureen," she said, "because we are staying right here until your son gets released."

Grandma scowled but said nothing. I thought about protesting, but I knew it would have been futile. Maybe I

could have left if Adam would call me back—he'd offer
to pick me up if I told him where I was, I was sure of it—
but my phone remained frustratingly silent. So I just
pushed two chairs together and curled up in them.

When I finally fell asleep, way past three, I dreamed
that I was a contestant on *Dancing with the Stars,* but I had
shackles on my legs and handcuffs on my wrists. The
host, Tom Bergeron, told me that I'd gotten confused—
that I was really supposed to be on his other show, *America's Funniest Home Videos.* The judges each gave me a two,
and then I looked down and realized that I was naked.

I awoke in the morning with a stiff neck and breath so
bad I could have used it as a weapon. Hunter lay curled
up on the floor nearby, lightly snoring, his head resting
on a stack of mug shots.

"Don't you dare wake him," my mom said. She was
still drinking the bad government coffee, and I wondered if she'd ever closed her eyes at all. "Maybe he'll
sleep until we get home and I can tell him it was all just
a bad dream."

I tiptoed over my brother and went to the window.
Outside, the early August sun shone cheerfully, brutally,
on the parking lot full of squad cars. I looked down at my
cell phone. Nothing.

"Morning, folks. How are you today?"

I turned to see a young and very cheerful policeman grinning at my grandma, who waved a knitting needle at him threateningly and said, "Get to the point or I'll slit your throat."

The cop looked taken aback.

"Ignore her," my mom said, taking a sip of coffee and gagging slightly. "She's still half asleep. I promise you she's incapable of violence."

"Try me," I heard Grandma mutter.

"Okay, you want the point," the cop said, still eyeing Grandma warily. "I can appreciate that. So here it is. Basically, to bail Mr. Malby out, you're looking at fifteen thousand dollars."

"What?" my mom yelled.

The cop smiled gently. "Though there are other options. He could stay with us until trial."

"Stay in the slammer? Fifteen grand? What are we going to do?" My mom clutched at the Styrofoam cup as if it were a life raft.

I couldn't believe it myself. It was like Mom said—my dad wasn't a criminal, he was just a moron. And that moronicness (yes, I know that's not a word) was about to cost us more money than they had paid for my entire college education, thanks to my scholarships and my work-study job in the rare books room at the library.

My grandma stood up and tightened the belt of her robe around her waist. "Well," she said, "let's get out of here. Let's go home."

At that my mom turned on her. "You sit right back down, Maureen. You're going to take care of this. Now cough it up."

My grandma raised her eyebrows until they disappeared beneath her powdery blue hair. "Whatever are you talking about, my dear?" she asked innocently.

"Don't 'my dear' me," my mom said. "Cough up the cash, Mo. Pay the man."

Grandma scoffed. "You think I'd be living with you people if I had that kind of dough?"

My mom grabbed one of Grandma's knitting needles and pointed it at her. "Yes, I do, because everyone knows you're cheap as hell. So knock off with the 'I'm a poor little old lady' crap, and bust into that giant wad of cash everyone knows you keep under your mattress. Not to mention in coffee cans and sock drawers and in the accounts at Citibank and God knows where else."

My grandma raised her eyes to the heavens, put her hand on her heart, and sighed dramatically. "Dear God, one day let my family love me for my soul instead of my remarkably elegant possessions, my shoe box full of cash, and my outstanding high-interest-rate bank account . . ."

Hunter, who had until then been sleeping soundly—or

at least pretending to—sat up suddenly and said, "I love your soul, Grandma!" And he wrapped his arms around her knees.

You've got to give the kid credit. Grandma melted.

"So," she said, turning to the cop and pointing her knitting needle at him again, "can I write you a check or do I need to hand you a suitcase full of unmarked bills?"

CHAPTER 21

My dad hung his head out the window, gleefully smelling the air just like a great big balding Labrador.

"I'm free, I'm freeeeeeee!" he howled. "God, look at the sky! The trees! Look at that guy drinking out of a paper bag! Look how happy he seems! Look at those pigeons fighting over that French fry! What fun! I tell you, family, this experience has changed my life forever. Old Walter is dead. And New Walter would just like to say . . . I love and care about each of you so very much."

He leaned over and kissed my mom, who patted his knee gently and sort of patronizingly. I could tell she wasn't buying it. She thought it was cute, sure, but she figured the Old Walter would reappear soon enough. How could one night in the slammer truly transform her husband?

But there was no calming Dad down. "I'm a new goddamn man. And you know what? This is a new goddamn family! Sure, we have our problems. Maybe I'm too bullheaded. Maybe Ryden's unemployable and Hunter licks his friends. And maybe Grandma is . . ." He turned around and looked at her, and I watched as he remembered that he owed his freedom to her. "So kind and loving and . . . well, downright saintly."

Grandma sniffed. "It's a burden, it's true."

My dad raised his fist and pumped it, nearly hitting the ceiling. "No matter what, we're all in this together. We're a family, damn it, and it's time we started appreciating each other. We're the Malbys! And from here on out, it's Malby time!"

"Malby time," Hunter shrieked happily. "Malby, Malby, Malby time!"

My grandma shrugged *what the hell,* and she, too, started to chant, "Malby, Malby, Malby," and so did my mom, and after a few seconds I joined in. Because my dad had a point. None of us was perfect, but we were family. And that was what mattered, right?

We pulled into the driveway, still chanting, and as we got out of the car we all still felt giddy from team spirit.

Hunter danced up the walkway, thumbed his nose at the coffin (which my dad had moved into the garage after the Ubbins complained), and said, "Let's eat shitty waffles!"

My mom patted his head and ignored his use of the *s* word. "Why not?" she said. "Today's a celebration."

My phone vibrated in my purse then, and I dug frantically to find it. "Adam!" I said, just as soon as I had it open.

"I'm looking for Ryden Malby," said a cool, female voice.

"This is she," I said confusedly. True, I hadn't looked at the caller ID, but I'd been so sure Adam would call—I'd left him a dozen messages by now.

"Ryden, this is Barbara Snaff from Happerman and Browning."

"Oh, hi, Bar—" I said, my heart pounding. "I mean, hello, Ms. Snaff."

"I called to let you know that the position you interviewed for a few months ago has become available again."

"Really? Really?" I didn't know what else to say. I stared at my mother, who was looking at me expectantly. I couldn't believe it—the job was open again, and they were calling *me*? What had happened to Jessica? I knew I wouldn't be able to ask this question, but then in the background I heard Jessica's unmistakable voice. *You want to fire me? Fine! I don't care! This place is shit!*

Oh, I thought. So that was it.

"Ahem," Barbara said. "Excuse us. We're having a bit of a personality clash in the hallway, it seems."

I could feel the goofy, incredulous smile spreading across my face. "Are you serious? You're offering me the job?"

I'm sick of being worked like a rented mule! I heard from Barbara Snaff's end. I almost laughed. I couldn't believe Jessica had such a dark side—she'd always seemed so perfect.

My whole family was standing on the lawn, staring at me. "Well?" my mom mouthed, and I gave her the thumbs-up sign.

"The job is yours if you want it," Barbara said. "Can you start on Monday?"

"Yes, yes!" I said. "I would love it. Thank you so much! Thank you!"

"Certainly," Barbara said. "We're glad to have you on board. See you at nine A.M."

When I got off the phone, my mom practically pounced on me. I hugged her around the waist. "I got a job, Mom," I said. "I got *the Job!*"

My dad did his fist-pumping thing again, and then a few karate chops to the air. Pretty soon my grandma and Hunter started fake-karate-chopping, too, just to celebrate, and before I knew it we were all chanting again.

"Malby! Malby! Malby!" we cried, as Mr. Ubbin stood on his front lawn, garden hose in hand, looking positively baffled.

When we'd quieted down and my family went inside, I pulled my cell out again. Really, there was only one person I really wanted to talk to now. I just wanted to tell him the good news. I dialed and, unsurprisingly, got his voice mail. "Okay, Adam, the silent treatment is pretty fifth-grade of you, but it's effective. I'm dying over here. Call me."

A couple of hours later, still high from my unexpected employment success, I called Adam again. "Just call me when you're ready to talk," I said. "Okay?"

But I knew now that more drastic measures were required, which was why I called my dad into my room. "You owe me a favor," I said.

"I don't owe you shit," he said. Then he looked surprised. "Sorry, that was the Old Walter talking. What can I do for you?"

I thought for a moment about pressing my luck—like, maybe I could ask him to please get his junk out of my room, because I was really sick of the smell of stale popcorn and finding those little soldiers in my bed. But then I remembered that it wouldn't be my room for much longer, because now that I had the Job, I was going to be getting the Beautiful Loft Apartment. So I stuck with my original plan. "I want to borrow Hank Buckalew's ice-cream truck," I said, putting one of his figurines back on its shelf.

My dad folded his arms across his chest. "Even the New Walter is curious about that request," he said.

"It's for a friend," I said. "It's an important mission of apology. You understand that, don't you? After your jail-cell conversion and all?"

My dad smiled. "Sure, sure. I'll call the old bastard now."

My Escort, may it rest in peace, was not a great car. But it was a Rolls-Royce compared to Hank Buckalew's ice-cream truck, which lacked power steering, air-conditioning, or even a radio. Maybe the makers of such vehicles were afraid the latter luxury would interfere with that horribly annoying song that all ice-cream trucks are required to play out of their tinny megaphone speakers.

Anyway, I managed to drive the behemoth over to the park where I knew Adam played basketball with a couple of guys from his prelaw course, plus Julio from the taco stand. As I turned into the parking lot, a little kid came running toward me, waving a dollar bill, but I motioned him away and inched toward the court. I pulled up underneath a scrappy-looking palm tree and scanned the rapidly moving players for the one I was looking for. And then I spotted him.

Adam was on the skins team, and so he was bare-chested, and his tanned upper body glistened with effort as he dodged the guy trying to guard him. I watched as he caught a high pass, faked right, then ducked under another guy's arm for a smooth layup. Nothing, as they say, but net.

Watching his concentration, his confidence, it occurred to me that I'd never really seen him like this. I mean, it was always just the two of us together, and it was almost as if I didn't even believe he could exist without me. Like somehow Adam wasn't fully Adam unless he was with me. And how, I was beginning to understand, I wasn't fully myself without him. How could he ignore my forty phone calls? And how, after ignoring all those calls, could he then just come over to the park and waste on his friends? Was it as easy for him as it looked?

I wanted nothing more than to run up to him and have him smile at me and ask me some dumb question about which I'd rather be, a lamprey or a sea cucumber. *Whatever you want me to be,* I'd say. *I'm just so sorry.*

But I couldn't do that. All I could do was what I did next. I took a deep breath, started up the truck again, and turned on that awful song. None of the guys turned to look, and so I kept moving forward. I drove the truck up over the curb and kept inching toward the court.

Then a tall guy in a Lakers T-shirt noticed me, and I could see the look of confusion on his face. I grasped the microphone in my sweating palm.

"Someone once told me that every evil and terrible thing in the world is directly offset by one simple dessert," I said. My voice sounded appalling through the speakers, but what the hell. I leaned out the window, and in my outstretched hand I held an Eskimo Pie.

"That's the hottest ice-cream dude I've ever seen," said the Lakers guy.

Adam looked surprised, and then slightly appalled. He dropped the ball and then bent down to retrieve it. He seemed torn between coming over and pretending that he had no idea who I was.

"I'm really sorry, Adam," I said, my voice blaring out over the court.

"You know her?" the Lakers guy asked. "Does she have rocket pops? I dig those, man."

Adam just shook his head.

The speakers crackled. "Also, if you don't forgive me," I warned, "I will follow you everywhere you go, playing this horrible song, until you go completely insane." To prove my point, I drove all the way onto the court and proceeded to follow Adam in a circle as he tried to get away from me.

"Okay, okay!" he finally yelled. "Just . . . stop. Just make that fucking song stop."

"With pleasure," I said into the microphone. And then I turned everything off—music, mic, truck. I climbed out of the cab and extended my peace offering, the Eskimo Pie.

"Where in the hell did you get an ice-cream truck? Is that your latest job?"

"I borrowed it from a friend of my dad's," I said.

Adam looked incredulous. "You're crazy," he said.

"I know. And I'm so sorry I flaked on you. I know you would have never done something like that to me."

Adam stared into the air above my head. He still hadn't taken the Eskimo Pie and it was slowly melting into my palm. He was right there in front of me and yet I was missing him—missing him like I'd never missed anyone before. He wiped a bead of sweat from his forehead and then pushed his sandy hair out of his eyes. I wanted to reach up and touch his cheek. I wanted . . . I wanted . . . I wasn't sure exactly, but it was possible I wanted to kiss him.

"Really," I said. "I'm so sorry. And I wanted to tell you—" I think I was going to say something really important to him, something I'd never said before because I'd never realized it—something about the way I felt for him, and how it was new and wonderful and it surprised me. But he cut me off.

"I accept your apology," he said curtly.

I was taken aback. "But—"

"It's all good," he said. "Moving on." He dribbled the basketball, still not taking the Pie.

"No, you have to really let me apologize. Let me make it up to you. I mean, you can't let me off the hook so easily. What I did was terrible."

Adam glanced over his shoulder at the other guys, who were standing around watching us and not making any effort to hide their curiosity. "It's cool. But I really got to get back to this game, Ryden."

"Wait, wait," I said. I held out the Pie one more time but Adam didn't take it. "Do you want to, like, hang out tonight or something? Hey! We should celebrate. I didn't tell you, but I got that job at Happerman and Browning! Which means I can get that awesome apartment we looked at." I could hear the desperation in my voice. I just couldn't make him seem to care, and I didn't understand why.

"Yeah, well, I've got to be packing."

"For what? Are you going on vacation?"

Adam stopped dribbling and tucked the basketball under his arm. "I've decided to go to Columbia." His tone was flat. Dead.

I took a step backward. I felt like I'd been sucker punched. "What? You're going to law school? You're moving to New York?"

"Yep."

My mind was reeling, but I didn't want him to know it. I gave him a smile so big it hurt. "Oh, my God. That's . . . that's . . . that's so great for you. Congratulations!"

He nodded and offered a half-smile back. "Thanks. I think it'll be good." He looked back at his friends, and then turned again to me. We stared at each other for a minute as the awkwardness between us bloomed like some horrible flower. "So, I'll, uh, give you a shout once I'm settled in."

"Okay," I whispered.

"See you around," he said. And then he turned his back on me.

As I watched him start up the game again, I felt worse than I'd ever felt before. He was leaving me, just like that. He was beginning his own new life, and I wouldn't be in it.

Because I wasn't sure what else to do, I took a bite of the half-melted Eskimo Pie. I guess I wasn't too surprised when it didn't make me feel better at all.

CHAPTER 22

Two weeks passed without a single call from Adam. I knew he'd arrived safely in New York, because he posted a picture of his new apartment on Facebook. But that was it. And though I was liking my new job at Happerman & Browning, without Adam to share it with, somehow it just wasn't nearly as exciting.

I mean, when I had to get the lattes for the staff meeting or proofread the publicity materials or make copies of manuscripts, it was all fine. But who could I tell about the time that Barbara Snaff came out of the bathroom with her skirt tucked into her panty hose? Who would laugh with me about Rory Furman, the perpetually stoned mailroom guy who had dreams of being a professional parasailor? (Once, just on a whim, I'd asked Rory which he'd rather be, a raccoon or an opossum, but he blinked at me with red-rimmed eyes and claimed he didn't understand the question.) And who would care that Lloyd Darby, my boss, had a secret obsession—and I do mean *obsession*—with *Baywatch*, a show that had not been good in its prime and now, however many years later, looked completely ridiculous? I just didn't have the energy for it alone. And the Beautiful Loft Apartment had gone to a banker, so I was back to trawling Craigslist, this time for an apartment.

In better news, though, my dad had managed to hang on to the positivity he had discovered as the New Walter Malby. There were a few slipups, like the time he told Hunter that if he didn't quit banging on the television he was going to flush him down the toilet, but all in all, he was quite a different person. Or maybe it'd be more accurate to say he was still himself, but just happier. In any case, he was having the time of his life. He had repainted his study bright yellow—the color of optimism and joy, he explained—and created a small Zen garden on our back porch. He'd even broken out the old NordicTrack ski machine he'd bought back in 1985 so he could have a new body to match his new attitude.

Watching him now, as he huffed and puffed in our garage, dressed in a matching turquoise tank-and-shorts combo that did nothing to hide his ample gut, I realized that patience had better be a part of the New Walter, because the new-body project was going to take a long time. After all, two decades of macaroni and cheese casseroles and chili fries do not melt off after a night in jail.

Mom appeared in the doorway, the cordless phone in her hand. "Walter, your boss is on the phone. He says he got your mission statement, but he doesn't understand what you mean by 'reclaiming our spiritual supremacy in the duchy of Luggagedom.'"

Dad rolled his eyes, panting. "Tell him to keep reading. I'm in the middle of something critical. Tell him that when he gets to the part about the soul of the salesman and the universe of the market it'll all become clear to him."

My mom shrugged and turned back to the phone. "He can't talk right now, Bob. He's pretending like he's skiing."

"Have a little faith," my dad shouted after her retreating figure. He turned to me. "You should try this, you know. It's really exhilarating and it burns, like, a thousand calories an hour."

"I'd rather watch you struggle with it, thanks." I got myself a soda out of the minifridge near the garage door. "So what's your next project?" I asked. "What's the New Walter going to do with his life besides revitalize the sale of suitcases in the greater Los Angeles Valley?"

My dad grunted. "Time will reveal all." He wiped his brow and then started to fake-ski faster.

Hunter wandered into the garage, holding Larry the sock puppet, who was looking as good as new thanks to a pair of darning needles from my grandma and a promise from my dad not to tear him to bits again.

Larry popped up into my dad's field of vision. "When are you going to build my boxcar?" Hunter asked in the squeaky voice he reserved for Larry.

My dad didn't respond—he was in some kind of exercise nirvana or something.

Hunter tried his own voice. "All the other kids' dads are practically done with their cars." He waited for a minute and then went on. "I keep asking you to help me and I don't know why you wouldn't want to. This is a manly activity, Dad. Don't you want me to grow up manly?"

"Can't you see I'm busy right now?" my dad hollered.

Hunter's face fell. He turned away. "Forget it," he said. "Never mind."

My dad bit his lip, and his pace on the ski machine slowed. "Hold on, son," he said. "Dad just needed to fulfill his time quota." He held out his wrist, showing Hunter his giant new stopwatch, which was waterproof to five hundred meters in case my dad ever decided to go cave diving or whatever. Because who knew what adventures the New Walter would want to have?

"See?" he said. "We're all done now." He turned the machine off and stepped down, then went and knelt in front of Hunter. "When's the race again?"

"Saturday," Hunter said, picking at a stray thread on Larry.

My dad leaped up and clapped his hands together. "Well, all right, kid!" he yelled. "Let's get going! I'm going to make you a goddamn star!"

Hunter frowned, looking baffled at this sudden change in Dad's level of interest in the derby. "Huh?"

"Go get your mother and your grandma," my dad directed. "We're going to need every able-bodied Malby we've got."

My grandma, who had been rooting around in the flower beds just outside the garage, poked her head in and said, "I'm not able-bodied, so you can count me out."

"Nonsense, Ma, you're fit as a tiger. Let me hear you roar!"

My grandma giggled. "Meow," she said.

"Good enough!" my dad hollered. "Now let's get this thing built."

I managed to beg out of it, though. Since New Walter was still riding high on my fancy new job, he didn't really seem to mind when I told him I had manuscripts to read.

CHAPTER 23

I'd tried to decorate my desk at Happerman & Browning with a few homey touches: a vase of tulips, a picture of Hunter and Larry, a paperweight shaped like a hamster that Adam had given me. But it still looked small and bleak, sitting outside the big corner office of Lloyd Darby, Editorial Director.

Lloyd was very nice to me, and sometimes he even answered his own phone, allowing me to spend my time on the thrilling task of filing submissions, marketing plans, and profit-and-loss reports. He was always clear about giving me directions, so that, for instance, I did not order chicken on ciabatta for the lunch meeting, but rather chicken *salad* on ciabatta. Once when I cut my finger, he gave me a Band-Aid, and one day when I struggled to heave a huge stack of unsolicited manuscripts into the reading room, he called over another assistant to help me.

If this sounds like damning with faint praise, that's because it is. My job at Happerman was not really what I'd expected it to be. I'd been prepared to work my way up from the bottom (or almost bottom—at least I didn't have to start down in the basement with the chronically high Rory Furman). I knew I'd be the low man on the totem pole, tasked with mindless chores and general obedience. So who cared that Lloyd's chair was an eight-hundred-dollar Aeron, while mine was a sleek but extremely uncomfortable plastic number? And did it matter that Lloyd had a view of the Hollywood Hills, while I had a view of his big mahogany door? Not one bit. It was the proper order of things.

But the truth of the matter was, I had not been expecting to pick up Lloyd's dry cleaning, wash out his sticky coffee mugs, or pick a giant wad of green gum off the bottom of his shoe, all of which I was asked to do within the first two weeks of my employment.

I'd thought I'd be dealing with actual books, you know? It's not as if I expected to be editing the next Salman Rushdie novel or anything, but I thought they'd at least want me to go through what they called the slush pile, which was the giant heap of unsolicited novels and story collections from would-be writers all over the country. But as Lloyd had quickly informed me, reading was on my own time. Filing was on theirs. Answering phones was on theirs. Making copies was on theirs. And typing up meeting notes was on theirs. So I still read the slush pile, but only after working hours.

I felt some sympathy for Jessica Bard, who had probably experienced an even greater degree of surprise when it came to the gap between her talents and what was asked of her. After all, she was valedictorian! She was senior class president! And they wanted her to take six pairs of Lloyd's cashmere socks back to Nordstrom? I could just imagine her fuming, sputtering mad. Because underneath that sweet smile, there was a real shark, I knew it.

At the end of my second week, I asked Lloyd, as casually as I could, "So what happened to your old assistant?"

Lloyd looked up from an advance copy of a book he was inspecting. "Jonathan Micah Miller is too old to be a prodigy now," he mused. "So how do we market him? It was better when he was handsome. Have you seen him lately? He's very bloated."

"Um . . ."

"My assistant? Jessica?" He chuckled. "We had differing opinions. I thought we were giving her an excellent opportunity at a prestigious firm, and she thought she was

God's gift to our payroll. I thought she worked for me, while she thought she ran the company."

I leaned against his doorframe and smiled. "That sounds like Jessica," I said.

"Oh, you knew her?" His voice indicated only a mild interest in the connections between his underlings.

"Sort of."

"Well, you're much better," Lloyd said. "You're properly grateful. Handily subservient. And you don't complain about working absurdly long hours, unlike Jessica. She thought we should hire another assistant editor. I said, why hire two when one is cheaper?" Then he turned back to his advance copy of Jonathan Micah Miller's *All That Is and Shall Be,* and I was left to ponder his assessment of my personality. Properly grateful? Handily subservient? Was I supposed to take it as a compliment?

If only I could have called Adam to talk. I'd tell him that I thought I was going to be a tiger but I was really only a mule. Or a draft horse or an ox—something hardworking and underappreciated. Since he wouldn't take my calls, I Superpoked him on Facebook, but he didn't respond. I was hurt at first but then realized I couldn't blame him. I hated it when people threw a sheep at me or sent me a Zulu coconut or whatever the latest Facebook fad was, too. I mean, really, what a lame way to communicate.

It seemed that if I was ever going to hear from Adam

again, I was going to have to try harder. The problem was, I was scared. How do you tell someone that after fifteen years you finally understand what he means to you? How, after all those chances you had to kiss him, now that you couldn't, you finally wanted to? I didn't know if Adam was the man for me, exactly, but I hated not having him in my life. I hated that he'd given me a hundred thousand chances to love him and I blew every single one.

I sighed and brushed my hair out of my eyes wearily. I had to stop thinking about Adam. And I still needed to get my bangs trimmed, and I couldn't imagine where I was going to find the time. I spent all day filing and faxing and all night reading manuscripts. Which, by the way, were usually terrible. Because I wasn't given the books that agents sent in for possible publication. Oh, no—I was given the slush pile, which contained novels about space monkeys written by junior high science teachers and poetry collections written by people who couldn't spell the world "lyrical." ("Leerycal," one moron named Ty Marcus wrote.) I certainly wasn't going to find the next Jonathan Micah Miller in *that* heap of wasted paper. I wasn't going to find Jonathan Micah Miller after he got old and bloated, even.

But still, I kept on going, because hope is everlasting.

It was a Friday night when Lloyd walked by on his way out to some fancy book party, complete with free cocktails and cute little hors d'oeuvres, and patted me on the shoulder.

"Listen," he said. "I want you to sit in on the conference call with London on Monday."

Immediately my mood brightened. "Really? Great, I'd love to." I gave my keyboard a happy little tap. Maybe I was going to be moving up the Happerman & Browning ranks faster than I'd thought.

"Fantastic," Lloyd said, donning a fedora. (He fancied himself the Humphrey Bogart type.) "Have a good night. And try to get out of here by nine, okay? I mean, I'm all for exploiting you, but we're not paying you enough for you to live here." He winked at me and disappeared into the warm Los Angeles night.

As usual, I was the last one in the office, and as I sat there, reading a novel about a boy who uses his six arms (yes, six) to fight crime, the sun set in lovely pinks and reds and the streetlights came on a hundred feet below me. The air-conditioning in the office shut down, the janitor's whistle faded, and then there was nothing in the building but me and the fading hopes of these terrible aspiring authors. I took a sip of my cold, old coffee and felt like the loneliest person in the world.

I suppose that's what drove me to David's house. We'd said hi but we hadn't really spoken since the night I flaked on Adam, which I think was for the best. It seemed as if David and I were both floundering, which did not bode well for our relationship, whatever it was. After all, a drowning person is never rescued by another drowning person.

The other reason to go to David's was that my family had gone off to a movie, and I didn't want to spend the night sitting alone in my cluttered bedroom with a half-dead goldfish and two broken popcorn machines, trying to finish one of the puzzles my dad had left in there.

"Ryden," David said, opening the door to my knock and looking surprised. "Nice to see you. I thought you might avoid me forever."

Though I had in fact considered doing so, I pretended to think he was crazy for suggesting it. "What do you mean?" I asked. I held out a six-pack of beer I'd taken from my dad's stash in the garage minifridge.

"Thanks." He took two bottles out, handed one to me, and sat down on the porch, patting the seat beside him. "Well, I saw the . . . disagreement you had with your friend that night."

I nodded glumly. "Yeah. That wasn't so great."

"Is it all cleared up, though?" he asked gently. David seemed actually concerned, which was nice of him.

"No." I picked at the edge of the label on the beer.

"So that's what's bothering you now?"

I took a long drink and shrugged my shoulders up and down, trying to loosen the tension from the long hours in front of the computer. "I don't know. Nothing is, really. I mean, I've got an incredible job now—"

"Not PAing, I assume," David interrupted with a smile.

"No. I'm an assistant editor, or an assistant to the editor, I'm not exactly sure of my job title. What I am sure of is that I work my ass off. But I always expected to. I'm . . . happy," I said.

"Good for you," David said, clinking his beer bottle against mine. "So you found what you were looking for. I told you that you would."

"Yeah," I said.

"That's great." He sounded a little doubtful of my happiness, but he was polite enough to let my white lie stand.

"What about you?" I asked, leaning back and staring up at his wind chime as it swayed in the breeze. "Sold any Guacanators lately?"

David made his voice slick and smarmy. "Let me tell you about one of the greatest inventions of the twenty-first century: it's part vacuum, part mop, and part shower scrubber—and it's one hundred percent fantastic. Meet the VacMoSho, your one-stop cleaning tool, guaranteed to cut your chore time in half! Available now for three easy payments of—"

"Enough!" I cried, putting my hands over my ears. "I don't know how you stand it."

David picked up a pebble from the little rock garden by his porch and tossed it into the yard. "Well, I don't have to stand it much longer."

"What do you mean?"

"I'm going back," he said.

I frowned. "Going back? Going back where?"

"I'm moving back to Brazil." He gazed out onto our street, looking pensive. "When I left, I was so desperate to get out, so desperate to come to this country and do something with my life." He paused and then chucked another rock. "And here I am: I'm thirty-four years old, I've got this nice house, I've got a nice convertible. I've got a job that fattens up my bank account each month. I've got a guy who wants me to direct his first feature film—a great little independent documentary. And I've even got an Inflate-A-Couch, a Guacanator, and two VacMoShos in my garage." He laughed wryly. "But what's the trade-off? I haven't seen my family in ages, I hardly know my own daughter, and I come home every night to what? The ghost of my dead cat?"

I cringed a little then, but held my breath, waiting for him to continue.

He reached down and grabbed a whole handful of

rocks. "I guess the thing is, I finally realized that what you do with your life is really just half of the equation. The other half—the more important half—is who you're with while you're doing it."

At that, he flung the handful of rocks back into the rock garden. After a second you couldn't tell which ones had always been where they were and which he'd just tossed there.

I swallowed another sip of beer, and let his words sink in.

CHAPTER 24

"Jesus Christ!" someone yelled, startling me from sleep. I sat up in bed, wrinkled my nose at the eternal smell of stale popcorn, and waited for what would come next. I heard some banging, a few more select curses, and then silence.

I pulled a robe on over my nightgown and stumbled downstairs. Grabbing a mug of coffee from the kitchen, I wandered through the house. The TV was blaring Saturday-morning cartoons to an empty den, and my grandma's chair—the one she spent 90 percent of her days in—was unoccupied. A house of Lincoln Logs had been abandoned mid-construction, and the iron on the ironing table was still warm. Where was everyone? Maybe, I thought, the aliens that I'd wished for at Martin Black's party had finally arrived, but instead of taking me they had taken the rest of the Malbys, and now little green men were being harangued by my dad and threatened with knitting needles by my grandma. I sipped my coffee and wondered if that would be a good thing or a bad thing. Like, who should I feel sorry for, the aliens or my parents? Then I heard a string of expletives coming from the garage area and recognized my father's unmistakable howl of annoyance.

I walked outside. The sun was sudden and brilliant, and through my squinted eyes I saw my dad slamming the back doors of his Suburban and getting into the driver's seat.

"Ryden," he called, "get your clothes on! We're going to be late!"

I refused to be ruffled. "Late for what? It's a weekend. What is there to be late for?"

My grandma stood at the rear of the Suburban, dressed head to toe in some yellow silk outfit like a giant, ambulatory banana. "For the race, you dope!" she yelled. "Now Walter, you just back on up out of the garage. You got plenty of room, miles of room. Watch that side mirror," she said as my dad, in backing the Suburban into the driveway, ran over the garden gnome that Hunter had given him for Christmas. No one else noticed this, and I kept my mouth shut, not wanting to be the bearer of bad news.

"Race?" I asked.

Hunter stepped into my line of sight, looking better groomed than usual. His shirt was clean and his hair was strangely shiny and slick. "The boxcar derby," he said. "It's only like the biggest deal in the world for me. I bet Ronnie Masterson ten bucks I'd beat his ass and considering I only have six dollars and thirteen cents to my name it's really important that I beat him."

My mom beamed at him. "Watch your language, dear," she said. "You know, you look so handsome when you use my hair gel."

Hunter looked nervously at his feet. "I really want to win," he said.

I was about to say something like, "It's not whether or not you win, it's how you play the game," when Mom gave me a warning look. Hunter had never won anything in his life, and he certainly wasn't likely to today, considering he had our dad's mechanical skills and short attention span to depend on in the construction of his boxcar. I mean, okay, my dad had fixed my Escort—but then he'd run it into a tree.

Even though I wasn't feeling very optimistic about

Hunter's chances, I ran upstairs and got dressed like the good, supportive big sister I didn't try enough to be. By the time I came back down everyone was sitting in the Suburban, practically gnashing their teeth with impatience.

"What took you so long, Ryden?" my grandma said. "I thought I'd be buried by the time you showed up in your little sundress. I swear I can feel my body atrophying with every passing second."

"It wasn't that long," I said, clambering into the back. "And I just got up about ten minutes ago, so why don't you cut me some slack, huh?"

"You should hem that skirt," Grandma said. "Show some leg. God knows it's too late for me or Carmella to do that. Who wants to look at our saggy knees?"

Mom shot her a look in the mirror. "I do not have saggy knees, Maureen."

"Nonsense. Every lady over forty does. It's just the facts."

"Maureen," my mom said warningly, "I do not have saggy knees."

"Well, okay, baggy, then. You've got to admit that."

"I. Don't. Have. Saggy. Or. Baggy. Knees."

Grandma shrugged and gazed out the window. "If you say so."

"Women!" my dad roared. "Hush!"

They obeyed, but my mom reached over and touched Dad's knee as he pulled into the street. "Now is that the New Walter talking?" she said sweetly. "To me it sounds like the old one. And you know how we feel about him."

"You *married* him," my father said. "Now shut up and let Hunter concentrate."

And so we drove the rest of the way in silence, broken only by Hunter's nervous humming of "Row Row Row Your Boat."

The boxcar derby course had been set up on the wide, gentle hill of Jacaranda Street in Glendale, in a neighborhood of modest seventies-era ranches and bungalows. A few sets of temporary bleachers had been erected, and good old Hank Buckalew had staked out a corner with his ice-cream truck, happily dispensing dripping soft-serve cones and rocket pops to the throngs of sweating children. A man in a clown suit limped around passing out balloons—no, he wasn't Buckles the Begging Clown, thank goodness— while a lone, bored cop leaned against a lamppost, making sure no parental rivalries or sugar-addled kids got out of hand.

The scene wasn't nearly as crowded as my graduation had been, but there was that same sense of anticipation and apprehension. Parents were milling around, holding their children by the hand and taking pictures and making small talk. They were also checking out the competition, of course: was that big eight-year-old really only eight? Did that boy in the red shirt with the stern father look sneaky, as if he'd already cheated somehow? Hunter had told us about how one kid who'd won a national derby title a few years ago was later found to have used a secret electromagnet in the nose of his car, which pulled him to the finish line faster than everyone else.

"Make way for the senior citizen," my grandma hollered, wielding her cane like a weapon as she maneuvered toward the bleachers. "I need a place to rest my weary old bones."

Mom and I followed Grandma while Hunter and my dad disappeared into the crowd. "You just cheer really hard for Hunter, no matter what," Mom told me. "I don't care if he comes in last."

"That's right," Grandma said. "It doesn't matter if even that crippled clown beats him."

"We don't say 'crippled,' Grandma," I whispered.

"Well, what do you say? Gimpy? Deformed?"

I put my head in my hands. Really, there was nothing to be done about her.

My grandma persisted, tugging at my arm. "What do the young people say, Ryden? Broke-ass? Is that a popular term?"

"Mom, make her stop," I said, whereupon my mom distracted my grandma by giving her a pack of Rolos to eat and later pick out of her dentures.

We sat in the top row of the bleachers, and we watched as the fathers rolled their sons to the starting line, each boy in his little homemade car looking fierce and determined. The referee stood at attention with his flag raised and his eyes already on his watch.

Hunter wasn't among them, and I began to sweat. Had he had a nervous breakdown and crawled under the bleachers to cuddle Larry? Had my dad backed Hunter's boxcar into a tree? Leave it to the Malbys, I thought, to screw up something as simple as a boxcar race.

But just as I was preparing to disown my family forever for their weirdness, their inappropriateness, and their general incompetence, my dad and Hunter appeared over the crest of the hill. I heard the crowd gasp at the sight, and I got to my feet in wonder as I watched them approach.

Hunter was dressed head to toe in black leather, with a giant belt buckle gleaming at his waist. (Apparently the cops hadn't confiscated *all* of Buckle-O-Bill's prized possessions.) And my little brother was behind the wheel of a sleek, shiny purple contraption with flames painted up the sides and a hood ornament that looked a lot like Larry the sock puppet. *No,* I thought, *it couldn't be—*

"Yep!" my grandma yelled to all who cared to listen. "That's my grandson! And that's my coffin he's driving! Isn't that the greatest thing you ever saw? Goddammit, that's a Malby for ya! Go, Hunter, go!"

Mom and I started cheering Hunter on, too, but he didn't seem to hear us. We watched as his eyes narrowed and he focused on the race. I'd never seen him look so intense, and my dad, standing behind him, was frowning in concentration, too.

"On your marks . . . get set . . . go!" The referee fired his gun and swung his flag, and the boys were off.

Hunter was slow off the starting line (that would have been Dad's fault), but he gained quickly on the group in front of him, and pretty soon he was closing in on the leader, a boy in a black car painted to look like a Trans Am. We yelled as loud as we could as he passed the kid by and shot out way in front of the pack. All of us were screaming and waving our hands, and we laughed with shocked glee as Hunter crossed the finish line ten feet before anyone else.

"That's my boy," my mom said. "That's my little vampire!"

We watched as Hunter kept on going down the hill, blazing mightily on ahead.

"Isn't he supposed to stop now?" I asked.

Then we heard Hunter's faint scream as the car's brakes failed to work. I could see the levers—were those part of Dad's NordicTrack?—clatter into the street. Unable to slow down, Hunter and his purple coffin-car jumped the curb at the bottom of the hill, rocketed across the grass, and landed with a huge splash in the reeds of the Jacaranda Park duck pond.

A dozen ducks flew squawking into the air. The whole crowd drew in its breath. My grandma clutched her heart, and my mother started climbing over the other spectators in her haste to get to the wreck.

"Hunter," I squeaked, "Hunter!" I thought about all the times I hadn't played with him when he wanted me to, and all the questions he'd asked me that I'd failed to answer (though I'd never be willing to explain the whole David-and-Ryden-were-wrestling business), and I felt certain that some terrible harm had come to my baby brother, and that life would never be the same again.

But then, after an interminable moment, my brother stood up from the lake, dripping wet and covered in lily pads, and he waved his hand wildly. Behind him, the purple casket floated away into the middle of the pond.

Then everyone began to cheer, and I could feel Hunter's happiness all the way from where he stood, radiating over us like some perfect warm sunbeam. My dad rushed over to my mom, and they put their arms around each other, and even my grandma stopped her bitch-on-wheels act to beam toothily and offer everyone around her some of her Rolos. I almost cried right then. I was so relieved Hunter was okay, and I was so grateful to him for being alive. And I was grateful to my whole family, because yes, they were completely insane and totally embarrassing, but they were all safe and sound and they knew how to come together when it counted.

Half an hour later, as we watched a still-sopping Hunter proudly accept a trophy that was about twice his height, I saw, in the background, a mother consoling her losing son. They were standing near Hank Buckalew's ice-cream truck, which the boy pointed to hopefully. His mom smiled and stood up, and then she handed Hank some money and accepted, in return, an Eskimo Pie. She offered it to her son, who took a big, eager bite.

Every evil and terrible thing in the world is directly counter-acted by the joy of biting into an Eskimo Pie.

And suddenly it all became clear to me. As I watched the boy devour the treat, I understood that I had been fo-cused on the wrong things entirely. I wasn't going to find happiness and purpose in the slush pile at Happerman & Browning. Because what I wanted didn't have to do with the Next Great American Novel or the Beautiful Loft Apartment. It didn't even have much to do with the Plan as a whole.

As Hunter stepped down from the podium and ran to-ward us, I turned to my family. "Mom! Dad!" I said. "I've got something to tell you."

Hunter flung himself at my mom's legs, hugging them fiercely, and she bent down and hugged him back. Then, still laughing with glee, he went to hug my dad, my grandma, and then me. "I'm so proud of you," I whispered into his wet little ear. "You're a champion."

"I know!" he cried happily. "I know!"

I looked up to see my mom gazing questioningly at me. "What did you want to tell us?" she asked.

I bit my lip. It was such a big thing to say. But then I glanced over at the little boy one more time, and I took a deep breath, and I said, "I'm going to move to New York."

My parents stared at me, bafflement on their faces.

"New York?" my grandma said. (She was never at a loss for words.) "New York City? Why in the world would you want to do that? You'll get mugged the minute you step off the airplane! I tell you, the Big Apple is rotten to the core. I've seen it all on the news."

"Hush, Maureen," my parents said in unison, and I let out a surprised laugh. I was going to move to New York! I could hardly believe it myself. Yes, it was crazy, yes, it was insane—and thus very much like something my dad would have done, were he a twenty-two-year-old whose best friend and greatest love had decamped for the other side of the country. It was totally uncharacteristic of me. But it was oh so very *Malby*.

I held out my hand to Hunter, who reached up and

took it. "Come on," I said. "Let's go get you a treat from Hank Buckalew's ice-cream truck."

And hand in hand, we walked through the crowd in the bright, beautiful sun, both of us happy, both of us knowing that today was something special.

CHAPTER 25

Considering I'd hardly ever really unpacked (there wasn't the room, what with all my dad's junk in there), it wasn't too hard to throw my things into a few suitcases and zip them up. In an uncharacteristic fit of financial extravagance, my dad had gotten me new luggage for the trip, rather than make me use the pink and orange suitcases I'd picked out when I was eight. When I protested that they were too nice, he waved away my concerns. "Employee discount," he said. "And remember, we've reclaimed our superiority in the duchy of Luggagedom."

I grinned. "Whatever that means." I stopped taking

inventory of what to bring and looked at him nervously. He looked back at me with a similar expression.

"Are you sure you want to do this? Really, really sure?" His face was kind.

I nodded. "Positive," I said with more certainty than I felt.

"You don't want to think about it for another few days?"

"Nope." I was afraid if I didn't go now, I never would. And I'd spend the rest of my life wondering what would have happened if I had. *Which do you want to be,* I asked myself, *a fearless eagle or a safe, quiet little mouse?*

I sat down on the bed, brushing off one of the little soldiers that had somehow found its way onto my pillow. "Just out of curiosity, though, do you think I'm making the right decision?"

My dad smiled at me, and then knelt at my feet. "You know, ever since you were a little girl you had everything figured out. You were so good—you ate your vegetables, you got great grades, you kept your room neat and clean. I've always been proud of you for that. But I was also kind of worried. Because the world's a screwy place, Ryden. It doesn't play by the rules, even if you do. I mean, look at me, I tried to buy a bunch of belt buckles fair and square and I ended up in the slammer. The point is, you can never be sure of anything. You have to just try. You have to not be afraid to fail. So. Do I think it's a good idea for you to quit your incredible new job—the job you've always wanted—and leave behind the only family you have to move three thousand miles away to a place you've never even been before?" He paused, and I held my breath. "I think it's the best idea you've ever had."

I couldn't believe it. "Really?"

He nodded. "Really. And I think you're going to knock them dead wherever you are. You're just that kind of girl."

I bent down and put my arms around his shoulders. "Thanks, Dad," I whispered.

"And darling," my dad said, "you'll always have us, that's the important thing. And as far as jobs go? You can always find another one, even another incredible one."

I teared up a little; I couldn't help it. My dad had never been so honest with me before, and it was amazing. He patted my knee tenderly. Then he looked around the room, at all the crap he'd collected and everything I'd be leaving behind. "Hey," he said, "do you think if I clean this place out a little I've got enough square footage in here for a home theater?"

I laughed and punched him on the shoulder. "Well, you've got the popcorn machines," I said. "So that's a start."

And that's how I came to be in the Delta terminal in

LAX, gazing at the cover of *Us Weekly* magazine and wondering what it was that the world found so fascinating about Kevin Federline.

Of course I was also wondering if I'd done the right thing. Because Dad was right: spontaneity was not my nature. Barring the whole ice-cream truck adventure, I could hardly think of anything I'd done that was surprising.

Maybe that was because I'd had my fair share of surprises from my dad, and they were rarely that fun. Like the day he announced that he, at age forty-five, was going to become a black belt in karate, and promptly broke his arm in two places during his practice. Or the time he showed up at my middle school dressed as Sherlock Holmes and claimed he needed his Watson—*me*—to help him find his missing checkbook. Or the time he thought a good moneymaking idea was to breed and sell ferrets.

But, I reflected, idly turning the pages of *Us Weekly* to see which celebrity wore what dress better, my dad certainly lived his life to the fullest. He may have been a supreme embarrassment to his adolescent daughter on more than one occasion, but he was trying to make something of himself. Something that didn't involve just working his way up the corporate ladder. And there was definitely something admirable about that.

So what if I'd chucked the entire Plan to throw myself

at the feet of a man who wouldn't return my phone calls? It was time I started to understand that life was an adventure, and that risks were necessary. And once I took this risk, who knew what others I might take? Maybe I'd go skydiving or bungee jumping; maybe I'd sail around the world or become a rodeo queen or run away with the circus or shave my head or decide to teach English in Mongolia or—

Slow down, little pony, I told myself. *One step at a time. Let's just take this risk for now. It's big enough.*

And then, as if the universe had noticed my change of heart and wanted to register its stamp of approval, who should I see but Jessica Bard, looking elegant but extremely harried as she tried to hold a hand mirror up for a very haughty-looking woman who was walking toward Gate A20, talking on her cell phone, and applying lipstick simultaneously. "No, I said it had to be *mauve,* not *eggplant,*" the woman was saying. "Everyone knows Truman Capote was much more of a mauve type. Are you as stupid as you sound?"

I couldn't help but smile. That could have been me. That *had* been me, in fact, although Lloyd had certainly been nicer than that woman. But now I was going to be something else, and that thought kept me smiling throughout the entire flight to New York.

CHAPTER 26

Another thing you should know about my family is that they love Christmas, even more than they love Chinese buffets. On the first of December, my mom starts baking sugar cookies and gingerbread men. My dad hauls the colored lights out of the basement and spends most of a day untangling them and cursing. Then he goes outside and strings them up in the rhododendrons and the Japanese maples. My grandma knits us new stockings to hang every year, and Hunter goes crazy making paper snowflakes and signs that say REINDEER CROSSING. I get into the Christmas spirit by singing carols, even though I can't for the life of me hold a tune.

The year that I was nine (the year I asked for the collected works of James Herriot, author of *All Creatures Great and Small*), my dad decided that he wanted to cook the entire Christmas dinner himself. He bludgeoned my mom into agreeing to this plan, telling her that for once she could put her feet up and relax. When the day came, he wouldn't even let us in the kitchen. It was his dinner, he said, and he had it totally under control. He was wearing an apron that said WORLD'S BEST CHEF, which we all knew wasn't true. I mean, the man had a hard time making toast. But we left him alone with the groceries, because what else could we do? He shooed us away with a spatula any time we came close to the doorway.

Eventually it was time to eat, and so we all sat around the table and waited for my dad to bring out the feast. And he came out bearing this huge, fifteen-pound ham on a silver platter. It was the biggest hunk of pig I'd ever seen in my life. And it was perfectly cooked, glazed, and everything. He set it down in the middle of the table and said, "Ta-da!" And then he started carving into it with a knife as big as a scimitar. My mom, though reluctant to question his triumph, asked where the rest of dinner was. Where was the salad, for instance, and the potatoes and the rolls? And my dad shoved a giant hunk of meat in his mouth and said, "That? The rest of that crap's just garnish."

I think what he meant to say was: when you have the

thing you want, nothing else really matters. That Christmas day, all my dad wanted was a big, beautiful ham. And on this September evening, all I wanted was Adam.

I took a cab to the address that Mr. Davies had given me, and then I walked up four flights of stairs to knock on Adam's door. My heart felt like it was going to leap out of my chest as I stood there, staring at the doorknob as if I could will it to turn and let me in. After a few moments, the door opened, and there Adam was: tall, green-eyed, a little bit goofy, utterly perfect.

"I'm here because I miss you," I blurted out. "I mean of course I miss you, I knew I would. But it's not a 'We had some great times, let's keep in touch, pal' kind of missing. It's more of a 'can't eat, can't sleep, forget what it feels like to laugh' kind of thing." I took a deep breath. "Because not to be too corny or anything, but I kind of think you took my heart with you when you moved to New York." When Adam didn't say anything I looked at the floor and mumbled, "So yeah, I don't know, maybe I should look for it in one of your suitcases or something." And then I looked up again, and that's when I saw the pretty brunette who was curled up on the couch behind him. "Oh," I said, my heart suddenly plummeting into my shoes. "Oh, dear."

And that whole time, Adam was just staring at me incredulously. "Ryden," he finally said. "Wow."

But I had already turned around and was heading back the way I'd come.

That was the risk of the grand gesture, I thought. The risk that your beautiful surprise would go to shit.

Or, as I liked to say, go to *shitshitshit*.

"Ryden, wait," Adam called, but I didn't stop. My pretty new suitcases rolled smoothly behind me as I walked down the hall.

I'd just go straight back to Kennedy Airport and get on the next plane back to L.A. I'd be back so fast Lloyd Darby and Happerman & Browning wouldn't even miss me—they'd just think I was out sick.

But then suddenly Adam was there, standing in front of me, and he was reaching for my shoulders and peering into my face and saying my name over and over again. "Ryden," he said. "She's my cousin. Anna Davies. She's a senior at Barnard."

I let the handles of my suitcases go and they fell to the floor with a clatter. "Really?" Could it be true?

"Yes, really," Adam said. "If you want I can show you a picture of us when we were little as proof. Somewhere I think I've got one where we're running around the yard pretending to be monkeys . . ."

"Oh," I said, exhaling gratefully, "that's such a relief. Because moving in with you and your new girlfriend would have been a tiny bit awkward." There! I'd said it. I'd taken one risk to fly across the country and another, even bigger one to say that.

Adam stared at me, then looked down at my luggage. "You mean you've got everything in there?"

"Everything I need," I said. Then I reached up to touch his face. "Almost everything I need, that is."

Adam put his hand over mine. "Why are your lips so far away?" he said softly.

I took a step toward him. "I was wondering the same thing."

He leaned in to kiss me, and just before he did, I put my palm out and stopped him. "Wait."

"What?" he asked. He tilted his head, looking concerned.

I smiled. "I think I'm in love with you," I said.

And then he swept me up in his arms and kissed me, and I felt dizzy and thrilled. When he pulled away, he looked right into my eyes and said, "Well, I'm glad to hear that, Ryden Malby, because I love you, too."

CHAPTER 27

I don't necessarily need my books to have happy endings—
I mean, how good would *Madame Bovary* be if Emma and
the doctor had lived happily ever after?—but I guess I'd
have to say that it's nice when life has a happy ending.

A week later, as Adam and I sat on the floor of his apartment, eating Indian food from one of those indistinguish-
able places on Sixth Street, I felt like my happy ending was
also a beginning. I had a best friend. I had a boyfriend. I
had a cute little apartment on 118th Street and Broadway
(well, *we* had it). And I even had an interview at Random
House scheduled for next week.

"Which would you rather be," Adam said, stabbing a hunk of cheese from his saag paneer, "a deer or a squirrel?"

I tore off a piece of naan and dunked it in a little tub of raita. "That's a good one," I said. "I'll have to think on it."

"Don't," he said. "Let's never play this game again."

My phone rang then but I let it go to voice mail. I smiled at him. "Okay," I said.

"Did you know that in Ohio, it's against the law to get a fish drunk? Also, you're not allowed to hunt whales on Sundays." He grinned. "In Ohio, that is. Where there is no place to hunt whales in the first place."

I looked at him perplexedly. "What are you talking about?"

Adam took a sip of mango lassi and said, "Oh, they're just some laws. Just a few laws I learned about in law school."

"Well, it's fascinating stuff," I said. "And it seems like it would come in really handy."

"It will!" Adam said, stealing a bit of my naan. "Because it's our new game. It's called 'Who Can Come Up with the Stupidest, Most Random Piece of Information?'"

I rolled my eyes at him. "That sounds annoying and hard." But then one occurred to me, and I blurted excitedly, "There are 293 ways to make change for a dollar!"

He clapped his hands together. "See? I knew you'd get into it."

"Because you know me so well." I sighed.

"Yes," he said. "I do."

We sat in silence for a little while, just enjoying our dinner and each other's company. I'd always felt so comfortable around Adam, but this was like a whole new level of ease.

Adam got up to get us more napkins. Poking his head out from the kitchen doorway, he said, "Hey, don't you want to see who called?"

I looked at my phone. "My parents," I said, sighing again.

"Play it on speakerphone," he said. "I want to hear how the old Malbys are doing."

I looked at him doubtfully and stretched out my legs. He walked back into the room and grabbed one of my feet and gave it a little rub. "If you say so . . ." I said.

I pressed the buttons and my dad's voice came bursting into the room. (He always thought it was necessary to yell into answering machines for some reason.) "Hey! Guess who's paying you a visit next week? We found cheap-ass tickets. Really. That's what they're called and everything. Cheap-asstickets.com. Seriously, check it out. Hey, does Adam have a pullout? Grandma says she gets the bed because she's the oldest. She made that whole age-before-beauty argument, which I think is bullshit, but whatever, the woman did get me out of jail, so I guess I have to do what she says once in a while. Your mother is after me to give the goldfish away—she thinks I ignore Bubbles. But she sends her love. And Hunter says hi, too. He's here with me in the basement. I fixed one of the popcorn machines. Do you want it for your apartment?"

In the background I could hear my brother shouting, "Dad smells like Cheez Whiz!"

My dad grunted. "He's lying, I smell like Aqua Velva and Head and Shoulders and he knows it. All right, call back about the bed." And then he fumbled to hang up the phone, and before he disconnected, I heard Hunter say "Cheez Whiz!" again and my dad say "Give me that god-damn sock pup—" and then, click, they were gone, just like that, and it was just me and Adam.

Adam opened a beer for each of us and leaned back against the couch. "Next week, huh?" he said mildly. "I guess they'll be here for my show at Pete's Candy Store. Did I mention that Sam from Captain Corduroy is going to be in town? He's going to sing backup."

"That's great," I said, smiling at him.

He smiled back. "So, pullout shopping tomorrow?"

I scooted toward him and put my hand on his knee and squeezed it. I thought about what David had said—

about how I'd find what I was looking for. And how he was right. I'd found it, right here in this little room.

"Definitely," I said, and then Adam pulled me toward him and held me as the sun set over the Manhattan skyline. *Magic hour,* I thought, and then I closed my eyes and kissed him.